IN THE SHADOW
OF THE PALI

IN THE SHADOW
OF THE PALI

A Story of the Hawaiian Leper Colony

LISA CINDRICH

G.P. PUTNAM'S SONS / NEW YORK

Library of Congress Cataloging-in-Publication Data
Cindrich, Lisa.
In the shadow of the Pali : a story of the Hawaiian leper colony/Lisa Cindrich.
p. cm. Summary: In the late nineteenth century, twelve-year-old Liliha is sent to the Kalaupapa Leprosy Colony at Molokai, Hawaii, where she struggles to endure savage living conditions and people, as well as her own disease.
[1. Leprosy—Fiction. 2. Survival—Fiction. 3. Conduct of life—Fiction. 4. Kalaupapa (Hawaii)—Fiction.] I. Title. PZ7.M27713 In 2002 [Fic]—dc21
2001048127 ISBN 0-399-23855-7 10 9 8 7 6 5 4 3 2 1 First Impression

Dedicated to Dan Cindrich,
best friend and cherished husband:
May you always find the sunshine.

With thanks to all those brave individuals who read various drafts of this novel and offered such insightful guidance: Kathy Dawson, Elizabeth Hearne, Amy E. Brandt, Kristin Satterlee, Natalie Ziarnik, Tracy Kisler, Mary Anna Glenn, and Dan Cindrich.

And with gratitude to Tom Fleming, Judy Mathewson, Karen Dewitt, and Jim Grant, who always stand ready with words of encouragement and support. What would I do without you?

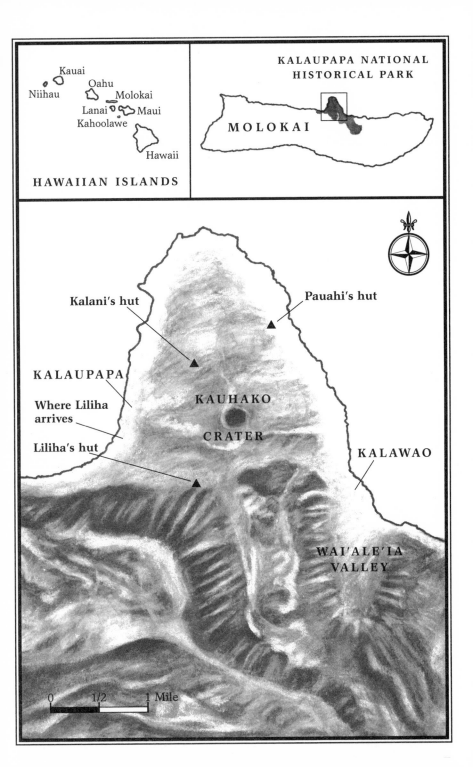

HAWAIIAN ISLANDS

Kauai
Niihau
Oahu
Molokai
Lanai
Maui
Kahoolawe
Hawaii

KALAUPAPA NATIONAL
HISTORICAL PARK

MOLOKAI

Kalani's hut

Pauahi's hut

KALAUPAPA

KAUHAKO

Where Liliha
arrives

CRATER

Liliha's hut

KALAWAO

WAI'ALE'IA
VALLEY

0   1/2   1 Mile

IN THE SHADOW
OF THE PALI

CHAPTER ONE

"WE'LL HAVE TO TAKE YOU IN ROWBOATS THE REST OF THE way," said the captain, striding down the deck of the transport ship. He stopped, glanced around; two dozen pairs of white, frightened eyes stared back at him. "We can't take this ship any closer to Molokai. Too many rocks. The surf is too rough."

Liliha leaned forward and squinted, trying to make the features of the island come clear. A dark wall thrust up from the even darker ocean. The wall must be the *pali,* she thought. The cliff rose behind Kalaupapa peninsula, separating it from the rest of Molokai island. The sea effectively formed the other three sides of a prison.

A prison for lepers. The officials at Kalihi Hospital and Detention Station near Honolulu didn't *call* Kalaupapa a prison. They called it a "colony" or a "settlement" or a "lazaretto." But Liliha knew better. When someone forced you into a place and wouldn't let you leave, that place was a cage.

The captain snatched a lantern from its hook and swung it toward the passengers. An old woman began to wail. Light flared through the glass panes of the lantern, striping the captain's cheeks and making his eyes gleam. He pointed to a skinny man with hollow cheeks and a scooped-out stomach.

1

"You. Get up." The captain nodded toward the rowboat hoisted along the rail. The skinny man slowly stood. He opened his mouth to speak, but the captain cut him off with a rough shove. "Move." The man's mouth shut.

"Come on," the captain snapped. "The rest of you now."

They rose slowly, one by one, gathering up their woven mats and cloth bags. Liliha only had the sack her mother had given her for the journey. Long and narrow, it was woven from kī leaves. A cord snugly closed the mouth. Liliha clutched the cord with one hand. With her other hand, she tightened a shawl around her shoulders. The pink shawl was her mother's prized possession, store-bought in Honolulu by Liliha's father back in 1850, the year her parents married and fifteen years before her father died.

Liliha stood. Her legs ached. She'd been on the ship since early afternoon. Now it was dark and had been for a long time. She'd hardly shifted position during the journey. At least she wasn't seasick like some of the other passengers. She'd always been a good sailor with a strong stomach, but the sore-pocked faces and swollen ears and stunted hands of those around her churned her stomach. She didn't want to look at them or to remember the terrible moment when the Scottish doctor at Kalihi Hospital had condemned her with a shake of his head and a single word: "leprosy." She'd had enough of the disease while taking care of her sick grandmother.

When she clambered into the rowboat, she banged her knee on a metal oarlock. Other people already occupied the four benches stretched across the boat. Liliha crouched on the floor. When she glanced up, she saw a sailor swabbing at the ship's rail with a wet cloth. It was strange how some of the sailors avoided the lepers while other sailors moved among them, unconcerned. A loud whistle sounded from the ship, and Liliha covered her ears against the shrill noise as the rowboat was lowered toward the sea.

With a slap, the boat hit the water. Liliha turned her head away from the sour-smelling puddle that slopped around her bare feet. A fine spray from the waves dampened her shawl and raised goose bumps on her arms. She'd promised herself she wouldn't cry. Uncle Malietoa had taught her—with harsh words and hard slaps—not to cry. Uncle Malietoa! This was all his fault.

A burly sailor lowered the oars and rowed. The boat bucked across rough, black waves much more turbulent than the surf at home. The wind was cool and gritty and stank of seaweed and salt. As the boat neared land, the *pali* loomed taller and steeper, blotting out half the night sky.

The boat came ashore, wood crunching against wet sand and rock. Holding a lantern, the sailor stepped onto land. "All right, then," he said. "Out you go."

Liliha peered up and down the shoreline. To her right, she saw a light, small and orange, glowing in the distance. To her left, half a dozen small wooden houses huddled together with a few grass huts. The Scottish doctor at Kalihi Hospital had told her that most of the sick lived near the water in a settlement called Kalawao, where there was supposed to be a hospital and food. The doctor said that they'd be given rations of clothing, too, skirts and blouses and even shoes. Shoes were something Liliha never wore and didn't want.

She nudged a man beside her. "Is that the village?" she said. "Kalawao?"

"Kalawao?" boomed the sailor, suddenly beside her. "Kalawao's on the other side of the peninsula. You can't see it from here."

"But the houses—?" Liliha pointed.

"Kalaupapa settlement. There are just a few people living over here now. They've always been here and they refused to leave when the government decided to bring in the lepers. The government says you aren't supposed to mix with them. They're not diseased." He tapped his skull. "Just sick in the head, if you ask me. Why anyone would *want* to live here . . ."

"But what about that light?" Liliha pointed at the orange light that had moved steadily closer.

The sailor flicked a hand dismissively. "Probably just some of *your* kind, come from Kalawao. They always keep watch for ships, especially when they know it's getting near time for rations." He nodded toward the light. "The road to Kalawao is that way."

"How far?" a woman asked.

"Three miles, maybe. Not far." He paused, his mouth drawing tight, covering his white teeth. "But a long way if you're one of those who has trouble walking."

As Liliha straightened her cramped legs and climbed from the boat, she stumbled. The sand wasn't fine and smooth like the beach at home, the kind of sand that warmed her feet and made her want to bury her toes in it. This sand was gritty and coarse, cold as a salt salmon just pulled from the ocean, and bristling with bits of rock and broken shell. Large black boulders littered the shoreline; some stood in dark solitude, others in ominous clusters with washed-up sticks and seaweed clotted around them.

The passengers watched as the sailor dragged the boat back into the water and headed for the ship.

"They're coming back," a man said. "One of the sailors told me so. They have to bring the rations."

The orange light had split into two, each growing steadily brighter. Liliha could tell now that they were lanterns. A voice shouted from that direction, a short angry bark that the wind shaved away.

The lanterns drew near, no longer seeming to glide, but stabbing forward and back, spotting patches of boulder and sand with light. Then, about twenty paces away, the lanterns stopped. Dark shapes bunched around the lights. Voices squabbled, fell silent.

Waves banged against rock; a startled cry burst from the throat of an 'ulili bird. One of the lanterns swung forward again. A face thrust itself into the light.

"Welcome to Kalaupapa." The words grated, low and hoarse, as if the lining of the speaker's throat had been scraped raw with a knife. The face looked like someone had taken that same knife and dug at the bridge of the nose and at each nostril, sliced at the mouth so that it opened in a black, perpetual gape, and pricked at the eyes until they oozed clumps of yellow-white pus. The stumpy figure pushed forward; when Liliha saw the ratty skirt dangling from the waist, she realized the person was a woman, a grown woman who only came up to Liliha's shoulder. A sickening odor permeated the air, and Liliha turned her face aside and gulped the seawind.

"So . . ." Another woman moved forward, raised a lantern. Her hair was cropped short, close to her skull. She wore a grimy white blouse with full sleeves tight at the wrists and a dark skirt that fell into shadow. Dark brown patches stippled her face, and her ears were soft and pitted as pieces of old fruit. Fleshy lumps rose from her forehead, and her lips were grotesquely swollen. A scar cut across one cheek.

"You'll love Kalawao," the woman said. Each word came hard as a rock from her mouth. "Won't they, Opuhumanuu?"

"Love it," her companion repeated, starting to laugh.

"Greatest place in the world."

The man nearest Liliha pushed forward. "They said the road to Kalawao is that way." He pointed.

"Road?" said the woman with the cropped hair.

"Isn't there a road to Kalawao?"

She regarded him narrowly. "You might call it that." Her mouth twisted just like Uncle Malietoa's when he gave one of his rare smiles. That same sly mouth with a fishhook curve to it. Sudden anger thrummed through Liliha's arms and legs, and she strode from the edge of the group until she stood directly in front of the woman with the shorn hair. Grabbing the lantern's handle, Liliha yanked it from the woman's startled grasp and raised it high, casting both herself and the woman into its circle of light.

"*Is* there a road to Kalawao or *isn't* there?"

She stared at the woman, who stared back with eyes the color of hardened lava. "It's my lantern," the woman snapped. She grabbed Liliha's free hand. The woman's hand felt rough and dry against Liliha's.

Liliha lowered the lantern. When she looked down, she saw that deep fissures cracked the flesh on the back of the woman's hand. Liliha let go so suddenly that the lantern nearly fell to the ground.

The woman pulled the lantern away from Liliha and raised it again. She leaned closer to Liliha. Her breath stank. "Don't you understand yet? You're nothing here."

The woman jerked away and stumped closer to the water. Opuhumanuu hunched along behind her, and another person—a man, Liliha realized, a man with a limping gait and a corrugated face—brought up the rear of the strange trio.

Dawn began to wash the shore with faint, gray light. Rocks protruded from the sand like broken teeth. Liliha slowly turned to face the cliff. Immense, its sheer vertical face hairy with green vegetation and sliced by occasional waterfalls, the *pali* reared up against the fading stars.

It looked far too steep to climb. A perfect prison wall. Liliha squinted. Near the top of the cliff was a sort of horizontal gash, thin and brown. Could it be part of a trail, zigzagging down the *pali* to the peninsula?

The rowboats pulled aground again, loaded with supplies. "*Pa'i 'ai,*" Liliha heard the woman with the shorn head say as sailors swung heavy crates from the bottom of each boat. *Pa'i 'ai* could be mixed with water to make a thick, sticky paste called *poi*. Liliha imagined holding a bowl of *poi*. Her head buzzed with hunger and her arms and legs seemed as light and wispy as stems of grass. She edged closer to the crates.

"Kalani," the dwarfish woman warned the woman with the cropped hair, pointing at Liliha.

Kalani whirled around. "*I'm* in charge of the supplies that come from Honolulu," she barked at Liliha. "The superintendent put me in charge. I pick up food for people who can't walk. I decide who gets what." Her eyes flicked to the side. "Opuhumanuu is just a helper." Her mouth curved into that sharp, dangerous smile again. "They won't have sent anything for you new people anyway."

Liliha didn't understand. "But they must have sent enough," she said. "We were on board. They know we're here."

"They never know anything," Kalani answered. "You might as well go on to Kalawao."

"*How?*" Liliha said.

"That way." Without glancing away from the crates again, Kalani jabbed at the air.

Liliha gave one last look at the crates and headed back across the beach to the others from the ship. "She said to go that way. The road to Kalawao."

"Do you think she's telling the truth?" a woman asked.

Liliha shrugged. If Kalani was anything like her uncle, she couldn't be trusted. Liliha could imagine Kalani setting them to wander for hours, lost, and smiling that thin, sly smile at the joke. Even worse, she pictured Kalani keeping bundles of food for herself while the newcomers bumbled their way inland. *They never know anything.* Suddenly Liliha had the feeling that

Kalani hadn't been talking about the government officials back in Honolulu. She'd been talking about Liliha and the others who were new to Molokai.

Liliha wavered. Should she go back over and demand one of the crates? But how would she carry it to Kalawao? The people there must have some sort of wagon to transport supplies to the settlement at Kalawao.

Yes, she saw a cart now, hammered together from rough, unpainted wood and pulled by a pair of scrawny horses that kept stretching their heads from side to side like they were seeking a chance to escape. Two men and a woman walked beside the horses, guiding them forward onto the sand. Rocks cracked and split beneath the wheels. The men and the woman looked healthy to Liliha. She wondered if they were *kōkuas*.

The Scottish doctor had explained to her that sometimes a leper's relative or friend agreed to accompany the leper into exile. These helpers were called *kōkuas*.

"Maybe your mother would act as a *kōkua* for you?" he'd asked. "It would be of great benefit to you to have someone help you with everyday chores, cooking, to nurse you as your illness progresses."

But when Liliha had pleaded, her mother's face had turned dark and her only answer was, "Maybe. We can talk about that later."

The people with the cart walked up to Kalani and began arguing with her. Then they took several crates and lugged them to the cart while Kalani watched with crossed arms and a bitter mouth.

So there *were* people to move food to Kalawao. Surely someone at Kalawao would provide a meal to the newcomers. Someone . . . of course. Kalani had mentioned a superintendent.

"I'm going to Kalawao," Liliha announced to the others. "A superintendent there runs the place."

"It only makes sense," an old man added pleasantly. He had a long white mustache and held the hand of a stout woman with thick, doughy skin. Wrinkles leaped like cheerful dolphins from the corners of her warm, black eyes. The man had the same discolored spots on his arms and hands that Liliha had, the spots that had made the doctor condemn her to this place. But the woman, most likely his wife, had clear skin. Maybe she was a *kōkua*.

The woman pointed past Kalani and Opuhumanuu, past the three people swinging crates onto the cart. "Ahia," she said to her companion. "Are you sure we should go to Kalawao? What about *there*?" She indicated the sturdy, whitewashed houses.

A man beside Liliha spoke. "One of the sailors said we aren't allowed to live there. The people in those houses aren't sick."

"We must go to Kalawao, dear," Ahia said, smoothing his mustache. "The road will take us there." Liliha followed his gaze. Near the spot where she'd first noticed the lanterns, she could now see the brown mouth of a road curving away from the beach. Ahia turned back to the group of newcomers and addressed them with the patience of a teacher. "I've looked at maps of the island. Molokai is shaped like a shark." He drew in the air with one slender finger. "The fin on its back is Kalaupapa peninsula. We're standing on the western side of the peninsula and Kalawao is on the eastern side." He pointed.

"So." Nodding, he started in the direction of the road. One by one the others followed.

Liliha took a couple of steps, then hesitated, looking behind her. Opuhumanuu squinted at her and gestured her closer with a crook of the arm.

Liliha stepped cautiously toward her, bent to hear Opuhumanuu's wet, clogged words.

"What do you think is waiting for you at Kalawao?" Opuhumanuu asked.

"A hospital. The superintendent . . ." Liliha faltered.

Opuhumanuu glanced at Kalani, who gave her a sideways smile and nodded.

"What?" Liliha said, her voice suddenly high and pleading, veering out of control. "What?"

"Haven't you heard about this place?" Opuhumanuu motioned Liliha nearer until their faces almost touched. Opuhumanuu's breath was even more sour than Kalani's.

"What?" Liliha repeated. Sweat sprang out on her face.

"A 'ole kanawai ma keia wahi," Opuhumanuu whispered. Liliha's stomach clenched and her chest tightened. "In this place there is no law."

Chapter Two

"Oh, yes, I've heard the rumors," Ahia said, smiling indulgently at Liliha, who strode beside him. The road was nothing more than two hard-packed parallel ruts worn into the earth. "I have a friend in Honolulu, very high up, an important man. Before I went to the hospital at Kalihi, I asked him what he knew about this place. Not rumors. Knowledge. Good solid facts. He said that it isn't a paradise, no doubt about *that*, but matters are reasonably well in hand."

Hana, Ahia's wife, nodded. Her smile was broad with an enormous gap between the front teeth. "Yes," she agreed. "Ahia's friend told us about one inspector—a man he knew personally—who came here a couple of years ago. It would have been 1867, I guess, and he said that, oh, there were a few things that didn't work so well, but overall—"

"Overall, it's going along fine," Ahia finished.

"Do you *really* think things will be all right?" Liliha asked, desperately wanting him to say yes, wanting Opuhumanuu's words to be a lie.

"Would I have voluntarily given myself over to the authorities at Kalihi if I didn't?" Ahia answered.

"You didn't try to hide?" Liliha had imagined that *everyone* tried to conceal the signs of illness.

"No, of course I didn't hide," Ahia said. "I had a strong sense of responsibility toward my neighbors. It was only sensible to separate myself."

"We lived in Honolulu," Hana added.

Liliha asked, "But, what about your children?"

"I'm afraid we were never able to have children," Hana answered. "Though that seems like God's blessing now. He knew what would be best for us. Still, I'll miss our neighbors' children."

"Better that we come here and leave them safe," her husband declared.

"Yes. What could be worse than seeing a child with such an illness?" Hana glanced at Liliha. "You're alone here?"

Liliha looked away. "My mother *couldn't* come with me," she said. "I have a brother at home." Now why had she said that? Her brother was already married and lived in a different village. But Hana's question made her feel ashamed, as if she had to explain her solitude, especially since she was the only child among the new arrivals.

"I didn't even consider for a moment staying behind while Ahia came here," Hana said. The morning sun had been out for a while now and was beginning to bear down. Hana swiped a wobbly forearm across her face. "You're not from Honolulu, are you?"

"No, a village," Liliha said. Sudden pictures of home rushed into her head: glittering beach, gentle surf, wind rippling through the palm leaves at night. Her mother . . . Liliha stiffened her throat muscles, holding back tears.

Hana said quickly, "How old are you, dear?"

"Twelve."

"A beautiful twelve-year-old."

Liliha's face burned and she stared at the road again. Beautiful? She was hardly that, and she knew it. She had a round face and puffy cheeks, eyes like small, black pearls beneath thick brows. A smattering of dots sprayed across her dark face. Freckles, the doctor at Kalihi called them, smiling and telling her about the freckled girls in Scotland, where he came from. Ugly, Grandmother had called them.

Liliha tried to smile at Hana, who was just trying to be nice, like most old women. But her mouth trembled. What did her fat cheeks and freckles matter now?

Hana said, "We'll check on you. Don't worry."

Liliha wanted to cry again. They would check on her? She knew what that meant. No matter how nice they were or how much they liked her, they weren't going to take care of her. *You have to take care of yourself,* she thought, swallowing her tears. *You should know that by now.*

"Anyway," Hana continued placidly, "you won't be alone here. No one is. Not really."

Liliha was confused. "I am," she faltered. "Alone." She wanted to see her mother with a sudden, fierce longing.

"I meant God is with all of us, always."

"Oh."

Hana patted Liliha's shoulder. "Things will be all right. God provides."

Provides *what*, Liliha wondered. Leprosy?

A few of the people who lived in Liliha's village were staunch Christians, always folding their hands and looking at the sky and parroting English words Liliha knew they didn't understand. Missionaries from the next village came to talk about that man named Jesus and to hand out small, black books that no one could read. Uncle Malietoa used his as fuel for the fire. Liliha's cousin tore out sheets, folded them into toy fish and gave an entire school of these paper fish to Liliha. When he'd found the paper fish, Uncle Malietoa had ripped them to shreds.

A few villagers were halfhearted Christians and even more were nothing at all. Hardly anyone kept the traditional, sacred taboos or danced to honor the ancient deity, Loki. Hardly anyone held to the old ways at all except Grandmother, who spoke with contempt of those who'd followed King Liholiho's commands and spent the last fifty years destroying *heiau* altars and violating taboos. "Men and women eating together! It's disgusting." Liliha remembered the revulsion on her grandmother's face. "Women devouring *bananas!*" Liliha knew one thing for sure: If Grandmother believed in the old ways, then she *never* would.

Ahia stopped so abruptly that Liliha nearly tripped over him.

A hundred yards ahead, the road curved behind a feeble gathering of *koa* trees. A slow line of people were shambling around the curve. As the first person neared, Ahia inclined his head and said, "Good morning." The woman didn't even look up. She wore a blouse identical to Kalani's, but even filthier.

Her dark gray skirt, made of coarse, nubby cotton, hung shape-lessly to the ground; the hem had come undone and the tat-tered fabric shivered in the dirt at each step.

Ahia greeted the next five or six people who tramped by, but when no one responded, he stuck his hands into his trouser pockets and dropped back to the edge of the road to let the pro-cession pass. Hana settled in beside him.

The first to walk by were tolerable, but the ones who came after, who were sicker and slower . . . Liliha recognized the signs of the disease; she'd seen the symptoms before, in the ruin of her grandmother's body and among the lepers who'd waited with her at Kalihi Hospital to be transported to the leper colony. Some bore only subtle symptoms: brown patches that appeared and disappeared; pale circles on the flesh; thickened, cracked skin; growths erupting from arms and legs or sprout-ing from the face; vanished eyebrows. Some of the sick creep-ing past her now were still more horrible to look at with their clawed hands, their feet worn to misshapen nubs. Several looked emaciated, with hollow chests, and others had earlobes so swollen, the flesh touched against their shirt collars.

Liliha couldn't look any more. She stared at the ground. Even so, she caught glimpses of stumps of feet stumbling past, heard the rhythmic crunch of makeshift crutches, smelled a foul odor of flesh rotting and was grateful for the wind that blew the stench away.

When Hana stepped forward and put her hand on a man's arm, Liliha looked up. "Where are you going?" Hana asked.

The man leaned against his single crutch. "A ship's come.

Just this morning." The cartilage of his nose was nearly worn away and his voice sounded clogged and stuffy as if he had a cold. "Didn't you hear the whistle?" He turned away before she could ask anything more. The worry that already fluttered in Liliha's stomach intensified as she watched the man walk away.

As they started down the road again, Liliha couldn't help wondering about some of the people who had passed them, people with such twisted and disfigured feet that walking must be agony. What would make them undertake such a long, painful trek? Maybe she *should* have stayed on the beach until someone gave her rations.

The abrasive smell of salt intensified again. They must be nearing Kalawao. Stone walls—tumbling apart, sprouting weeds—stretched across the land, sometimes veering near the road, sometimes winding *makai,* toward the ocean. Wind struck the weeds with a continual, dry murmur.

Ahia stopped once more to nod sagely and proclaim, "This must be it. Kalawao."

A whitewashed fence made of tall wooden pickets enclosed a small compound. Outside the fence was a field in which dozens of holes had been dug and filled. Liliha eyed the field. Were those holes graves? They were packed closely together, but each was about the size of a man. She shivered.

Inside the fence were half a dozen buildings constructed in the style of the *haoles,* the white people: The straight boards of each wall were interrupted by regularly-spaced windows and topped with angled roofs. A single *pū hala* tree twisted up from the dirt square in the middle of the compound. It was the only tree inside the fence and it only emphasized the starkness of the buildings.

Up close, the fence wasn't a crisp white, but a speckled gray. Some of the boards were rotted where they emerged from the ground. The buildings were dingy. Cracks threaded across windowpanes, each fracture a fine, dark scar. The central square was almost deserted. A man slept curled in the shade of the *pū hala*. A small boy, maybe six years old, crouched by the fence, poking at something with a stick. Liliha stared at him, then looked away. He was so young; he probably had a mother or a father nearby. Anyway, she told herself firmly, she didn't have time to worry about him. Not now. Not with hunger and fear gnawing at her gut. Where was the superintendent? Why didn't anyone come out to greet the new arrivals?

"Seems a bit . . . empty," Ahia remarked. Hana put her hand on his shoulder.

"Where are all the people?" a man wondered.

"Probably over getting food from the ship," Liliha blurted.

Ahia raised a finger. "I'm sure the superintendent is nearby. He'd have come to meet us if he'd known exactly when the boat was due to arrive. Now, which building . . . ?" Head cocked to one side, he turned in a slow circle.

Liliha's stomach cramped with hunger. The pain made her impatient and she stepped toward the largest building. If the superintendent was the most important person at Kalawao, he should live in the biggest house. Behind her, Liliha heard the others spread out, chattering anxiously. She pushed the door open and stepped inside.

The smell struck her first, a reek of rot and soaked bandages. At first she could only see dim outlines, but as her eyes adjusted, she made out more details. The windows seemed even smaller from inside, limp curtains obscuring the glass. Several shelves lined one wall; on them stood a few half-filled blue and green jars stoppered with corks.

Something moved on the floor. Liliha looked down. Through the gloom, she saw heaps of rags moving and realized that people lay beneath those tattered blankets and filthy clothes. There were no beds in the room, no pillows, scarcely any mats. She recognized immediately that these were the sickest, worse off than the lepers she'd just seen crossing to Kalaupapa landing. These were the blind, burning with fever, gulping each breath through open mouths, their muscles wasted, their hands and feet no more than lumps. She'd seen people dying of leprosy before, including Grandmother. These people were close to death.

One man groaned and raised himself onto his elbows. His blanket fell around his waist. Although his chest gleamed with sweat, he shivered as he reached to pick up a ladle beside a rusting metal bucket. He clumsily scooped the ladle into the bucket. Metal clanged. Liliha jumped at the sudden noise.

The ladle clattered onto the floor. Across the room, another man began to shift about, his legs stretching and retracting. A powerful new stench billowed up from his body.

Liliha bolted outside.

The compound was no longer quiet. Hana, Ahia, and the rest trailed in the wake of a stout *haole* man with graying hair and an iron-colored beard who wore a long blue coat of heavy cloth. He turned for a moment, his colorless eyes staring, unblinking, at the people following him. He said something—short harsh words that Liliha didn't understand. He stabbed a single, sharp finger into the air, shook his head viciously, and strode to a small building across the compound. The door to the house already stood open, and a boy, not much older than Liliha, waited beside it until the man thudded up the two steps and disappeared inside. The boy vanished after him, and the door shut like the jaws of a shark.

Liliha ran to join the others gathered around Ahia. "What is it? Who was he?" The questions stumbled from a dozen mouths. Confusion clouded Ahia's face. His mouth worked soundlessly.

"That was the Captain," Hana said gently. She paused. "The superintendent."

Voices erupted, shaking with outrage and fear. "That was English, wasn't it?" a man said. "Can't he speak anything but English?"

Hana shook her head. "I'd guess not."

Liliha pressed to the front. "What about food?"

Hana glanced at her husband. "He said that there are no extra rations for us here."

"But the supplies that came today . . . ?"

Hana briefly shut her eyes. "People who can walk are there now, collecting their rations. The cart will bring some supplies for the very sick, the people in the hospital." She pointed at the building Liliha had mistakenly entered.

"But not for us." Liliha's words tasted flat and dry.

"No."

Ahia gave a sudden, determined tug to the silky white hairs of his mustache. "This is outrageous. They can't mean to leave us here to starve. That certainly isn't what the authorities in Honolulu intend. The man is an incompetent. It's astonishing that they would put him in charge."

"Talk to him," Liliha urged. "You have to explain to him. Please." If only she spoke English herself! But her stomach flip-flopped at the thought of arguing with the impatient man in the blue coat.

Ahia glanced from Liliha to the door guarding the Captain's house. Maybe he felt the same fear that Liliha did. He lowered his gaze, just for a moment, then raised it again. His face cleared.

"Yes," he said, starting forward. "Of course."

Hana and Liliha followed. It *didn't* make any sense. Putting someone in charge who couldn't speak the same language as the people he was supposed to help? Kalani's words erupted into Liliha's thoughts: *They never know anything.*

Ahia stared at the door, his hands limp. "I do wish the Captain had seemed more . . ."—he considered a moment—"more hospitable."

Liliha swayed on her feet. She thought she heard a strange, hollow sound rush into her ears, a roar like that held within the spirals of a conch shell. When had she ever been so hungry in her life? Never. Not even when Uncle Malietoa, to punish her for being too slow to weave a new mat for him, refused to let her eat or drink for an entire day.

In desperation, Liliha reached around Ahia and knocked at the door. No one answered. She jiggled the knob until rust stained her hand.

She knocked again, her hand banging wildly at the wood.

"Liliha." Hana's large, warm hands enveloped her own. "Listen."

Footsteps padded behind the door. A moment later the door inched open. The same boy who had vanished into the house behind the Captain now leaned out and looked around with dark, questioning eyes.

"Where's the Captain?" Liliha blurted, furious that the Captain was hiding from them, avoiding the people who needed his help. Hana swayed up beside her, smiled benignly, and said, "We'd like to speak with the superintendent. Is this where he lives?"

The boy slowly nodded. "This is his house."

Hana's smile grew radiant. "And is he home now?"

Liliha was wild with impatience at the question. Of course the Captain was home! Hadn't they all just watched him go inside?

The boy glanced over his shoulder. The angle of the door concealed most of the room.

"Is he home?" Hana repeated amiably.

"Yes."

A moment passed. "We'd like to see him, please."

The boy glanced down, his feet shuffled forward and back. "All right. He might come out."

"We would prefer to come in."

The boy gnawed at his lower lip, which was already chewed and bloody. "All right." He shuffled backward, pulling the door open.

The Captain's heavy wooden chair seemed to fill half the space. He sat tall against the back, his arms running the length of each rest, his hands gripping the rounded ends. The room was sweltering, especially after the boy shut the door again. Shutters pulled across the windows let in wedges of sunlight that filtered yellow and dusty through the air.

Ahia bowed awkwardly as if he'd forgotten how to do so. Hana nodded pleasantly. Liliha stood with her hands clenched behind her back.

"Ahia." Hana motioned her husband forward. With small, birdlike steps, chin bobbing up and down, he picked his way closer to the Captain. His voice was quiet and deferential, the Captain's answer loud and gruff. As the conversation continued, Ahia spoke less and less until the Captain made a final, harsh pronouncement, jerked one hand at the door, and turned toward the square table wedged beside his chair.

"Manukekua," the Captain called, and the boy came forward, lit the wick of the lamp that sat on the table, and fixed the lamp's glass chimney back into place. The light flared a moment, then settled into an irregular flicker that illuminated the objects cluttering the table: an open ledger with stained pages, tins of tobacco, loose sheets of paper and a pen fallen across them like a spear. The boy slipped into the back room and returned with a stout pewter mug, which the Captain yanked away from him.

"Ahia?" Hana said, her hand gentle on her husband's shoulder. They went outside. Liliha started to follow them, but suddenly spun toward the boy, Manukekua.

"None of us has eaten since we left Honolulu," she told him.

Manukekua watched her carefully as if she frightened him a little. Were her eyes wild? Was her face crazy? Living in a place like this, he'd probably seen lunacy before. Liliha noticed for the first time a sore that opened a small wound high on Manukekua's cheek, near the corner of his eye. She saw no other sign of the disease. If his ears were swollen and pitted, the coarse black hair falling past his jaw hid their condition.

At last he said, "The rations came today. At Kalaupapa landing."

"You don't have any food here?" Liliha's voice thinned to a whisper.

Manukekua's glance flickered to the Captain, who was draining the contents of the pewter mug. "Not much."

"What are we supposed to eat?" Her voice broke, but she held his gaze until he looked away.

"I'm sorry," he mumbled.

When the Captain banged the empty mug against the table, Manukekua went to the back room and emerged with an ornate bottle glowing with amber liquid. Neither he nor the Captain glanced at Liliha. She rushed from the room.

Ahia and Hana stood with the twenty-one others at the break in the fence where the road ran from the compound. Ahia's thin shoulders slumped toward his chest and he pressed one hand absently over his mouth. Hana's plump face was solemn.

"No," she said to the other new arrivals. "There's nothing here. I'm sorry." She whispered something to Ahia.

He nodded and lowered his hand from his mouth. "My wife and I are going back across to the landing site. All the food is there."

When the crowd milling around Ahia broke into more questions, he flung his hands out. "That's where the food is. The less time wasted here the better." He caught Hana's arm; together, they pressed their way onto the road.

Hana turned and called back, "Come with us. Believe me, the Captain said there's no food for us here."

"Unless the Captain's lying," the man nearest to Liliha muttered through his teeth. "Or *they* are." He nudged his chin at Ahia and Hana. "How do we know what the Captain really said? I bet there are storerooms in some of these buildings."

Hana looked directly at Liliha. "The food is back where we landed. I promise you, that's what he told us."

Liliha almost followed. Surely Hana was telling the truth. But the Captain had looked so strange, so uncontrolled; there might be a calabash of *poi* ten feet from him and who knows if he'd even notice? She couldn't just tag after Hana, expect the woman to take care of her. Hadn't Hana already as good as admitted that she didn't want to take responsibility for Liliha? That she only wanted to check on her occasionally?

Liliha shook her head at Hana, who frowned and turned forward again.

Then from down the road came the wagon. Dust billowed up from the wheels and the horses' hooves. Ahia stopped to watch it pass, but Hana took his arm and gently tugged him into motion again.

The wagon creaked into the compound and stopped at the hospital. "They haven't brought much," a man muttered with disappointment. On the wide wagon bed, the low stack of crates looked ridiculously small. Liliha and the others gathered beside the wagon. The woman riding on the cart jumped down. Ignoring the newcomers, she opened the hospital door and propped it wide with a stone. The two men clambered from the wagon and hoisted crates to their shoulders. The woman threw one anxious glance at the hungry faces of the onlookers and hurriedly followed the men inside.

"We could go in, too," a man said. "See where they're stashing the stuff."

Liliha stared at the crates still loaded on the wagon. What if she just *took* one? Just walked off with it right now before anyone returned from the hospital? Who would interfere? Who would punish the theft?

Not that it would be theft. Not really.

Liliha hesitated. The woman came out of the hospital and positioned herself beside the wagon as if she'd guessed that the supplies were threatened. She stayed there while the two men carried the rest of the crates inside. Not looking at anyone in particular, she announced, "This is for the patients in the hospital. It's little enough as it is. You'll have to make do until the next shipment."

"But when will *that* be?" someone bleated.

"I don't know. They don't come on a perfect schedule. A couple of weeks probably."

A man behind Liliha started to cry, a horrible, rasping noise. Liliha's hands rose to her own face, but she was too angry to cry. She glared at the Captain's house. He knew they were out here, hungry and tired and scared.

"Maybe there's still food back where we landed," a woman with wide, frightened eyes suggested.

"No," said the woman at the wagon, still not meeting anyone's eyes. "It'll all be taken by now."

"We should have stayed at Kalaupapa," a man spat. His face and hands were covered with sores, and his fingers were already shortened and beginning to look as if they were fused together. "Damn that Ahia anyway." He mimicked Ahia, pretending to pull at a mustache. "I have friends in *very* important positions," he said, clipping his words. "I'm practically a *haole,* don't you know?" Shaking his head in disgust, the man stalked from the compound to the road.

At first, no one moved; then, as if invisible bonds broke, they scattered, some running to the road, others storming into the hospital or banging on the door of the Captain's house.

When Liliha slipped out of the compound, no one saw. No one cared. Taking a deep, shaky breath, she strode out across the rough ground, her bare feet sweeping like scythes through the grass.

CHAPTER THREE

WHEN SHE CAME TO WHAT LOOKED LIKE AN EMPTY HUT A good quarter mile outside the compound, she stopped. It was small and crude, windowless, with a low grass roof. Mold fuzzed the thatch, and a ragged square of cloth billowed in a doorway so squat that anyone but a young child would have to stoop to pass through it. Liliha knew what such huts were like inside: damp, earthen floors; musty air; leaky roofs.

Any people who lived there were well hidden.

Or they're coming back from Kalaupapa landing with food, jeered a voice in Liliha's head.

Behind the hut she found a halfhearted garden. Someone had cleared a small square of land, and a few pallid leaves shaped like arrowheads sidled up from the earth. Liliha crouched, ran her fingers along a stalk: thin, dingy, and pale green. *Taro?* Weak, sickly, and dried-out, yes, the stalk pitted with holes where some insect had attacked it, but *taro* nevertheless.

From *taro* she could make *poi.* She glanced around. Two people were coming across the field, but they were still far away. The hut remained silent.

Liliha dug quickly with her fingers. The stalks broke, but she kept digging until she'd cleared out the area around each bulbous root and forced the plants up from the soil. The bulbs were small and hard as wood, but she stuffed them into her sack without taking the time to knock the dirt from them. She glanced across the field again. The people were closer. What if they were the owners of the hut, returning home with their rations? Her heart tripped into a sick, unsteady rhythm. She stuffed one last plant into her sack, smeared her hands across the front of her skirt, and crept closer to the hut. She felt terribly visible. If only there were more trees, more places to hide.

She glanced around the side of the hut, slung her sack easily over her shoulder as if it held nothing she wished to conceal, and stepped away from the building's protection. She forced herself to walk calmly across the field until, finally, she couldn't stop herself from glancing at the people coming still closer to her.

She sucked in her breath. Kalani! How could she not have recognized the woman's aggressive gait, the way she stamped each foot down as if it were a stone grinding into a *poi*-pounding board? Opuhumanuu followed Kalani. Even at a distance, Liliha could feel Kalani's poisonous stare. Liliha wondered where the man had gone. Probably to hide the crates of food they'd looted.

Liliha veered sharply off and rushed away from Kalani. It would make her appear afraid, but she couldn't stop herself. She *was* afraid. She didn't want to meet up with Kalani again, not yet, not when she had some food in her sack but was still half-dizzy with hunger. When she finally let herself look back, Kalani and Opuhumanuu were small figures receding in the direction of the compound.

Liliha clambered across a stone wall and flung herself down beside it. She snatched at the mouth of the sack, drew it wide, and plucked out the first plant her fingers touched. The root was hard and she had no pestle, no *poi* board, no calabash or water or fire. She managed to dent the skin of it with her fingernail.

She glanced left and right, raised the bulb to her mouth, and bit at it. It hurt her teeth, forcing her to nibble until she was able to get a tiny pinch of meat into her mouth, along with a grudging sip of juice. Despite the bitter taste, she continued to swallow small shreds of *taro*. The food did little to blunt her hunger. She leaned against the wall and pushed the *taro* into the sack. She pulled her arms around herself. If she were at home, oh, if she were at home, her mother would take that *taro*, scrub it clean, cook it until it was soft, mash it with water to make a good *poi* paste. Liliha closed her eyes and remembered the slightly tangy scent of her mother's skin, the simple grace of her hands as they mended a shirt or braided rope or combed hair.

She remembered the last time her mother had made her favorite food: coconut pudding. That was three months ago, when Grandmother still had a good two months to live. Liliha pushed the sudden image of Grandmother from her thoughts. She concentrated instead on making the picture of her mother come clear.

Uncle Malietoa was the only brother of Liliha's dead father.

Uncle Malietoa's hut was the largest in the village though it still consisted of a single, windowless room. At dusk that day, Liliha's mother had sat outside the doorway mending a fishing net that Malietoa had torn the previous morning. Liliha had squatted beside her. The earth had been cool and soft against Liliha's bare feet, and the evening breeze had been warm. She'd glanced at Grandmother's hut, considerably smaller and danker, that stood twenty feet away. Grandmother had fallen asleep in the middle of criticizing Liliha's "untidy hair" and "rude voice." Liliha was glad that Grandmother was getting sicker and weaker; the sicker the woman got, the more she drifted off into sleep and into strange, semiconscious states. And that meant Liliha had more freedom to sneak away and visit with her mother and, sometimes, with her cousin who was only a year older.

"Where is Uncle?" Liliha had asked, watching her mother's plump fingers effortlessly weave new cord across the ragged hole in the net.

"With the other men." Liliha followed her mother's gaze past the other huts. On the beach a fire glowed orange against a purple sky and darkening ocean. "Drinking. Acting like fools." She spoke without rancor.

"As long as he stays away," Liliha observed.

"That's right." Her mother held the net up for inspection. "How is your grandmother today?"

"Worse. But that doesn't stop her from yelling."

Her mother lowered the net and began working at it again. "How are her eyes?"

"I look at them and I think she must be blind—or almost

blind. But then she starts to complain and it's like she can see *everything*."

Her mother hesitated. Finally, she ventured a question. "Complain?"

Liliha's hands flew out in frustration. "The water was too hot when I tried to wash her. Her food was cold. First, my voice is too quiet, so she can't hear me. Then it's so loud, it hurts her ears. She says we're taking food from Uncle Malietoa and we'll never be able to pay him back."

Her mother shifted uncomfortably and stared at her work. "Well, in a way that's true, Liliha. We can't really repay Malietoa. And he *did* take us in after your father died."

"And you do all the chores and I spend all my time in *there*." Liliha pointed at Grandmother's hut. "Doesn't that count for something?"

"What else can we do?" her mother said quietly. Setting the net aside, she stood and stepped through the doorway, gesturing for Liliha to follow.

The hut's interior was spotless, the dirt floor swept clean, the woven sleeping mats neatly stacked, the table, single chair, and oil lamp faintly gleaming in a shadowy corner. Liliha's mother took a small clay pot from the table, removed the lid, and held the pot close to her daughter's face. Liliha breathed in.

"Coconut pudding!" she said.

Her mother nodded. "Malietoa got into it already, but I really made it for you." They grinned at each other. "Go ahead, Liliha."

Liliha scooped two stiff fingers into the pot. She closed her eyes, savoring each sweet, cool mouthful; when she opened them again, her mother was watching her. Although her mother smiled, her eyes were sad. Liliha's hand paused above the pot.

"Go on." Her mother nodded. "Finish it up."

"But Uncle . . ."

Her mother's gaze flickered toward the doorway. "It's all right. Go on."

Liliha needed no more encouragement. Her fingertips slid along the bottom of the pot, swiping up every last bit of the pudding. Coconut pudding *was* a treat, not so unusual for Malietoa or his daughter or even for Grandmother, but rare indeed for Liliha.

"And your own—" her mother began, stopped. Liliha licked the last of the pudding from her fingers until the skin was glistening and smooth. She looked up. Her mother was trying to smile, and failing, her lips quivering. "And your arm?"

Liliha wiped her fingers against the front of her dress and pulled her sleeve back from her wrist to her elbow. Her mother bent forward to look. The last evening light coming into the hut was weak, but the two pale circles on Liliha's forearm seemed almost to glow, white discs against dark skin.

"They're bigger," Liliha said, letting the sleeve fall back into place.

Fear and some other obscure emotion mingled in her mother's face, turning her cheeks a rough crimson. "Do you feel all right?" she asked Liliha.

Liliha nodded. "Yes, but . . ." After a moment's hesitation, she spoke quickly. "Do you think it's the same as Grandmother's?"

The thought that she might suffer from Grandmother's disease made her go light-headed with fear.

Her mother pulled her into an embrace. "No. No, of course it isn't. People get odd marks and blemishes all the time. There's nothing strange about it." Her mother pulled back her hair to reveal a squat black mole on one side of her neck. "This just popped up last spring. Who knows why?" Her arm tightened around Liliha's shoulders in an almost-painful grip.

Liliha closed her eyes and tried to let her mother's words convince her that she was healthy. She could smell her mother's skin and the coconut on her own breath. Her mother's warmth was comforting. The worst of Liliha's fear gradually dissolved, though a tough root of unease remained.

"Here you are!" Uncle Malietoa's voice was as thin and sharp as his face. He pounded across the room, grabbed Liliha's arm, and yanked her away from her mother. "Your grandmother is calling for you and here you are gabbing and gossiping with this woman and—and—" His nose wrinkled and he stared at the empty clay pot on the table. He turned to Liliha, his gaze like a flaying knife. "Did I say you could eat that?" Picking up the pot, he slammed it down against the table. "Did I?"

Liliha managed to shake her head.

Liliha's mother, standing behind her, murmured, "I told her she could, Malietoa. It was my fault."

His stare snapped past Liliha's shoulder. "That's right. It *was* your fault. *And* the girl's."

Not a sound from her mother. Liliha couldn't even hear her breathe.

Malietoa's eyes cut at Liliha again. "Your grandmother's waiting for you, girl. She's *been* waiting."

Liliha tried to hold his gaze, but couldn't. She offered him a single poisonous glance before running out of that hut and into her grandmother's hut.

Grandmother was sitting up, her back against the grass wall, her shriveled legs protruding from beneath a crumpled blanket. A small oil lamp burned beside her. She turned her cloudy eyes to the doorway as Liliha slipped inside.

"Worthless thing!" Grandmother thrust a wooden comb at Liliha. The comb had a curved handle and graceful tines. Liliha had carved it for her own mother, who, at Malietoa's command, had handed it over to Grandmother.

Liliha knelt beside the woman and began to comb her limp, white hair. She combed it every morning, but somehow, by nightfall, there were always knots and rat's nests. Sometimes Liliha suspected Grandmother of deliberately snarling her hair just to give Liliha another unpleasant chore.

"I've been calling for you," Grandmother stated, closing her eyes and leaning her head toward Liliha, who tried to work the comb through a particularly stubborn tangle. "You were ignoring me. Don't tell me you weren't."

"I didn't hear you," Liliha answered honestly.

"Hmm! I don't know who's a more disgusting liar, you or your mother. Ouch!"

"Sorry." Liliha drew the comb free. Anger bubbled like lava in the pit of her stomach. She could take insults. No matter how unfair they were, she could swallow them down and survive. But when the insults were aimed at her mother . . .

She set the comb down. "Do you want to look in the mirror?" she said, keeping her voice sweet as she reached for the pewter hand mirror set in the corner with Grandmother's other treasures. The pewter was elaborately ornamented with curlicues and swirls. An admirer of Grandmother's beauty had given it to her when she was fifteen years old.

"Phaw!" Grandmother clawed the mirror away. It was no wonder she didn't want to see her scarred cheeks, her nose that resembled candle wax melted and solidified into a grotesque new shape. The mirror struck the floor, sending up a thin poof of dust. "Do you think you're so pretty?" Grandmother said. Her breath, fetid with the odor of brown, rotten teeth, pressed against Liliha's face. "Because *you're* going to look like this. Oh, yes." Grandmother's eyes were malevolent. Liliha shrank away. "I can still see well enough to know what's happening to you. I've seen your arm."

As she fled outside, Liliha could still hear Grandmother's laughter. She ran past villagers sitting outside their huts in small, neighborly groups, gossiping and joking. A couple of them waved at her, but Liliha didn't have any friends because Uncle Malietoa wouldn't permit it.

At the beach, empty except for outriggers and nets stowed above the tide line, Liliha threw herself on the sand. She lay on her back, listening to the sound of her breath and staring at the sky. Thousands of stars pulsed against the darkness.

Grandmother couldn't be right. She just couldn't be.

Liliha pulled back her sleeve, held her arm above her face. In the darkness, the skin looked almost black, untainted. She told herself not to worry, but the fear was like a parasite, crawling inside of her, out of her control.

And she was right to worry, of course.

Grandmother told Malietoa about the marks on Liliha's arm. The villagers had let Grandmother live in peace in her own hut. They would have done the same for Liliha, but Uncle Malietoa reported her to the missionaries the very day after Grandmother died, and the missionaries reported her to the police. Once Grandmother no longer needed her care, Uncle Malietoa couldn't get rid of Liliha fast enough.

The policeman who transported her to Kalihi Hospital had been pleasant; the doctors—especially the Scottish doctor—were kind, but there was no cure, not even a serious treatment to attempt. The doctors offered no hope at all.

Did the disease enter her as she ate the remains of Grandmother's meals from the same bowl? Or did it come during the long hours suffocating in Grandmother's hut, breathing the same fetid air, combing Grandmother's hair, cleaning her sores, and laying wet cloths on her face whenever the fevers came? Since the age of seven, Liliha had spent her days caring for Grandmother. Five endless years.

As the doctor pronounced his verdict—"exile"—Liliha swore she would never again let someone bully her the way Uncle Malietoa and Grandmother had. She'd obeyed them and look what that got her: disease and banishment. Never again.

A sudden blast of wind, cool and wet, jerked Liliha from her memories. Storm clouds massed overhead. They cast a murky green light across the peninsula that made it impossible to tell afternoon from evening. Liliha shivered. How long had she been sitting there, lost in thought? She scrambled to her feet.

She opened her sack, her fingers scrabbling past the gnawed *taro* to reach her pink shawl. Pulling it out, she scowled. The weave was too loose to actually provide any warmth. Why hadn't her mother made sure she had a *real* shawl, or, better yet, a blanket?

She gripped the scalloped edges together in front of her chest. She'd brought so little with her: the shawl, a hair ribbon and comb, a skirt and shirt given to her by a woman at the neighboring mission. The missionary had also given Liliha the long navy skirt and baggy white blouse she wore now. No more loose dresses or capes made of *kapa* cloth. *"Why, it's no better than paper!"* the missionary had exclaimed. *"Imagine making cloth from bark! You need to dress properly now."* Liliha looked at the desolate fields around her. What did it matter what she wore here? She wished she had one of her own dresses again, loose and comfortable. But her mother had stored those away on the missionary's advice.

Liliha was famished again, her stomach turning inside her like a small, clawed animal, but she wanted *poi,* not raw *taro.*

She looked toward the compound. Was that smoke rolling above the fence? She sniffed the air in alarm. Had one of the buildings caught fire? The hospital?

Liliha pounded toward the fence, the sack banging against her leg like a warning.

CHAPTER FOUR

THE HOSPITAL WASN'T ON FIRE. NOR WERE ANY OF THE other buildings. Near the center of the compound, just far enough from the *pū hala* tree so as not to threaten it, a small bonfire crackled. Liliha stopped by the fence and stared.

Apparently, people had returned from the landing site with their rations; they'd gathered near the fire. She recognized some of the people who'd come ashore with her. They were the ones begging scraps of food, and not very successfully. She smelled the sour odor of beer, a familiar aroma. Uncle Malietoa and other men of the village used to make it from *kī* leaves and would get drunk in the evenings. She recognized the way the men here sprawled laughing around the fire, the way they watched certain women. Liliha was suddenly glad she was only twelve and looked young for her age.

She edged closer. Three men and two women sat in a circle and watched with glittering eyes as one of the men dealt cards from a ratty deck. On the ground lay a heap of objects: a wooden bowl, a grimy shirt, a stubby cigar, a brick of *pa'i 'ai*, a pair of coins.

Liliha stepped nearer to the fire. A withered-looking woman crept beside her. The woman held a shallow bowl and, with her other hand, scooped *poi* onto her fingers, then licked them clean. The woman smacked her lips.

Anger surged through Liliha. That *poi* belonged to her just as much as it belonged to anyone at Kalawao. She wanted to knock the bowl from the woman's hands. Better to splatter the food on the ground than let anyone else eat it.

If only she'd just stayed at Kalaupapa landing until the rations were given out! But would Kalani have let her have any? Liliha snorted and shook her head hard, almost startling the woman with the *poi* into dropping the bowl.

Liliha's face flushed hot and she patted the sack against her thigh. Was it stealing, taking the taro? When the Captain did nothing to provide food, but let Kalani take whatever she pleased?

Liliha turned to stare at the woman with the bowl of *poi*. She could take it from her. She *could*. That's what Kalani would do. That's what people here did.

The woman, feeling the intensity of Liliha's gaze, glanced up and, alarmed, dropped her head down toward the bowl again and ate with frenzied haste. She wouldn't meet Liliha's eyes.

Liliha slumped and turned away, went to the fire and, crouching beside it, pulled the *taro* from the sack. She couldn't eat the bulbs entirely raw, but how could she cook them? Simply thrust them into the flames? She had to have a pot of water.

She walked in a slow circle around the fire. She saw a metal bucket, the rim eaten jagged by rust. A woman sitting by the bucket shifted toward it, her arm reaching to pull it to her in a protective embrace, but Liliha lunged at the bucket and grabbed it away.

"That's mine!" the woman cried.

"I'll bring it back," Liliha muttered, turning quickly away.

The woman scurried after her.

Liliha ran her fingers along the sticky inside of the bucket, scooping up the remaining rice and devouring it. The woman was still staring at her. "I just need to borrow it," Liliha said, and stepped away. The woman watched with dumb, disbelieving eyes and continued to follow, but at a distance.

Liliha nearly tripped over a man passed out on the ground. He held the handle of a mug loosely in his fingers and, when he snored and shifted position, beer slopped over the rim. Liliha gently drew the mug from his hand and poured the beer into the bucket. When she bent to replace the mug, she glanced at the man's face gleaming in the firelight. She grimaced at the thought of that oozing mouth set against the mug, sucking at the very beer she intended to cook with. She crouched by the fire, dropped the *taro* into the bucket, pushed it close to the flames, then leaned back to wait.

To one side, a man and woman kissed noisily and sprawled laughing on the ground, the woman kicking her legs up into the air so that her skirt flopped around her thighs. Liliha looked away. On her other side, the card game continued with angry mutterings and squawks. The shirt, the bowl, the cigar: Each had moved to a different pile now.

Liliha took her second skirt out of her sack and wound the fabric around her hand like a thick mitt. She nudged the bucket away from the flames. Steam, sour-smelling as the beer, seeped over the rim. The leaves from the top of the *taro* plants were limp and pale, much of their color bleached. Liliha plucked a leaf from the bucket, blew on it, and chewed. Bland. She ate a second leaf, and a third, chewing furiously, her head down. When she reached for a fourth, she stopped herself. Her hands hovered just above the rim.

Had Hana found anything to eat at Kalaupapa landing? Or would she and Ahia come back to Kalawao tonight, hungry?

Liliha peered at the mess of leaves in the bucket. A sudden fierce joy blazed through her, joy that Hana and Ahia had gone off and she didn't have to share the food with anyone. She could eat more, then, couldn't she, and *maybe* save a bit for Hana, just in case? She reached into the bucket again and again, her hand never hesitating now, until the worst of the ache left her stomach. She ate all the roots, softened by cooking though still tough and hard to chew and with none of the goodness of *poi*. She peered into the bucket. Only a few wilted leaves swam in the murky beer. She plucked them out, wrapped them in the skirt, and pushed the bundle into her sack. She glanced back to see the woman who owned the bucket still watching, still cowed.

Liliha stopped. What if she kept the bucket? The woman looked so weak, her eyes hollowed and her mouth etched with lines of exhaustion. Liliha ran the fingers of one hand along the bucket's broken rim. It was sharp in places and the rust felt like moss. A bucket or a pot or even a bowl would come in handy.

Her jaws clenched. Why hadn't her mother thought to give her a pot and a bowl to bring with her? Why didn't her mother predict the need for such things? Liliha shook her head in anger although part of her knew the anger was unfair. Her mother had assumed that, of course, the settlement would provide such necessities. But a hair ribbon? A lace shawl? Still, her mother had treasured that shawl, kept it safe, never dared to wear it. And she'd given it to Liliha without hesitation. Liliha's anger faded.

She heard a strange noise and looked up. The woman was inching closer, making a pleading sound low in her throat.

"Oh, here!" Liliha burst out, shoving the bucket into the woman's startled arms. "Take it!" The woman clutched the bucket to her chest and gawked. "Go on," Liliha snapped, and the woman sidled past the card players and disappeared into the mob.

Liliha was still hungry, and angry now, too. What was wrong with the superintendent that he provided nothing to his charges, that he allowed conditions where people could fight over a rusty old bucket?

"Opu!"

Liliha spun around at the sound of that harsh voice. On the other side of the fire, through wavering flames, Kalani stood with fists dug against her hips, looking at Opuhumanuu.

"Opu," Kalani repeated slowly. "You know you can't drink all that at once. You'll drown yourself." Her voice was scratchy, like she'd been breathing in the smoke of the fire for hours. Liliha shrank farther back, peering from around a pair of drunken men.

Opuhumanuu took a deep, noisy breath, raised a cup to her lips, and tried to chug the contents. She sputtered and coughed.

Kalani laughed and stepped away, staggering a little. She stopped beside a woman who sat, cross-legged and hunched forward, near the Captain's house. Kalani prodded with one foot at the woman's knee.

"What is that?" Kalani said.

The woman bent her head lower. Though her hair hung around her face, she was obviously eating something with desperate haste.

"What *is* that?" Kalani leaned down and snatched something from the woman's hand. It was a chicken leg.

Kalani hissed, "Where did you get this?"

The woman didn't answer. Kalani raised the chicken to her mouth and began to tear a long, luxurious strip of flesh with her teeth, but she stopped when the door to the Captain's house swung open. The Captain seemed to fill the doorway. He stared straight past Kalani, past the fire. Liliha twisted around to see what he was looking at, but there was nothing except storm clouds building over the shadowy ocean.

Abruptly, Kalani was in motion again, holding the chicken triumphantly above her head, chewing with her mouth open. "Haven't you learned anything yet?" Kalani spat at the woman curled on the ground in front of her. Then Kalani drew her leg back and kicked the woman hard in the ribs.

Liliha cried out, a strange, strangled sound, and took a step forward. Too late. Kalani's foot connected with the woman's ribs again, in precisely the same spot. Liliha heard a crack. The woman moaned and pulled herself into a ball, shielding the damaged ribs.

Kalani tore the rest of the meat from the chicken and threw the gleaming bone onto the ground. She turned her head to stare at Liliha with hot, triumphant eyes. Hardly breathing, Liliha fell back a step.

"Opu!" Kalani grunted. "Bring me *kī* beer! We're not *allowed* to brew *kī* beer, are we?" As she said this, she watched the Captain, who remained, rigid, in front of his house. "Go on. Get me some!" Opuhumanuu hunched over with a gouged wooden cup and held it out to Kalani. Kalani snatched it and drained the contents. Then she extended the cup toward the Captain. He still looked through her, but suddenly swung away from the house and strode across the compound, past the fence. Liliha thought she saw him stumble once and wondered if he'd already sampled the *kī* beer himself.

"More." Kalani flung the cup at Opuhumanuu, who scuttled off with it in search of more beer. "Captain Do-Nothing. Captain Know-Nothing. Fool." She prodded with one big toe at the woman curled in the dirt. The woman gasped and crawled away. Kalani watched with disdain as the woman dragged herself out of sight behind the Captain's house.

Kalani threw her head back and barked, "Opu! Where *is* it?" She stalked toward the fire, where Opuhumanuu was trying to swipe a man's beer to pour into Kalani's cup.

Liliha saw that many of the men and women shrank away as Kalani passed, trying to make themselves obscure, unnoticed. Liliha was ashamed to find that she shrank back, too, afraid of the violence in Kalani's eyes.

The door to the Captain's house eased open. The boy, Manukekua, slid through an opening just wide enough for his thin shoulders. His gaze darted across the compound, caught Kalani and Opuhumanuu beside the fire as Kalani raised her cup to down another swig of beer.

Manukekua leaned forward and gestured for Liliha to come closer. They both kept their eyes on Kalani. Manukekua's sunken chest made him look even skinnier. He ducked his head and whispered, "There's some food in the Captain's house. It belongs to him, it isn't mine, but I could give you something really fast. I don't think he'd notice if it wasn't too much." He shifted from foot to foot.

"You didn't offer me anything to eat earlier."

Manukekua gnawed at his lower lip before he finally answered, "I couldn't. Not with the Captain there."

"You do whatever he says? Anyway, I already found something to eat." She forced her thoughts away from chicken, eggs, sweet potatoes, coconuts.

"Did you see which way the Captain went?" Manukekua asked.

"Why? Do you have to go fetch him?" Manukekua flinched. Liliha felt vicious. Maybe it was fear that sharpened her tongue.

Now Manukekua wouldn't even glance at her. His cheeks burned red. "I should go find him," he mumbled.

"Why?"

"He—so he won't get hurt."

Liliha turned away angrily. "So what if he gets hurt? What does he do here anyway? He doesn't give out any food. He doesn't make sure people have houses."

Thunder rumbled, the sound low and muffled, hidden deep inside the clouds. Liliha looked at the fire and the people sprawled around it. Where would they go when the storm struck? To the huts she'd seen scattered across the peninsula? Hana and Ahia rose quickly into her thoughts; she wondered if they'd made it back to Kalaupapa landing.

Pointing, she said, "He went *makai,* toward the water." Then she shoved past Manukekua and out of the compound.

She needed to find shelter. Maybe some of the scattered huts were empty, maybe even the hut where she'd found the *taro.* In the near dark, the peninsula was even more desolate. Liliha shivered, wishing that even one window or doorway glowed with lamplight to welcome her. At the same time, she was afraid to go near any hut that was already occupied. What if she entered Kalani's hut by mistake?

She nearly fell over a tumbledown wall.

Squinting down the length of it, she saw a large, dark shape trembling against the stones.

She didn't realize it was a makeshift tent until she stood beside it. Someone had anchored one edge of a ragged blanket to the top of the wall with loose stones, then stretched the opposite edge of the blanket down to the ground and fastened it there by pressing sharpened sticks through the cloth and into the earth.

Liliha bent forward, but pulled abruptly back when she heard someone inside the tent cough. She glanced at the clouds. What kind of shelter was this? Rain would soak the blanket, make it so heavy, the entire tent would collapse.

Another cough ripped at the tent. Liliha's face stiffened. She smelled something, an odor that made her think of the hospital. Then the wind pushed the odor away, replacing it with the cool, clean scent of rain. Liliha's skirt flapped like an angry goose at her legs.

The person inside the tent groaned and turned. A toeless

foot wormed from between a pair of the wooden stakes, loosening them until they tilted at crazy angles.

Liliha bolted across the field. Where was the hut with the *taro*? The garden had looked untended. Abandoned. Was it nearer to the *pali*? Or closer to the shore?

Scattered raindrops became a fine drizzle that grew steadily denser and colder. Although Liliha put her head down, rain caught at her eyelashes.

The hut was closer to shore. It had to be. She veered in that direction, her head bent and her eyes squeezed half-shut.

Someone stepped in front of her so suddenly that Liliha stumbled. She raised her head and peered through the darkness at Kalani's hard face.

CHAPTER FIVE

KALANI POINTED AT LILIHA'S SACK. LILIHA GATHERED IT
close to her side and took one step to her left. Kalani stepped
in front of her again. Liliha's jaws clenched so hard that the
bone ached.

Kalani nodded at the sack.

"What do you want?" Liliha asked. She shifted the sack behind her. "It's mine."

"Yours? Like the food you were eating tonight was yours?"

"And the chicken *you* ate?" Liliha's voice trembled.

Kalani's hand pressed toward Liliha's face. Liliha turned her
head to one side.

"I saw you steal," Kalani said.

Liliha saw herself, too, crouching in the garden, rooting up
the *taro*. How much had Kalani witnessed from a distance?

"I didn't take it from anyone," Liliha protested.

"*Taro* doesn't grow wild here. Especially not in gardens."

"Who said I had *taro*?" Liliha asked. If only she could keep
her voice steady.

"I saw."

"Like I saw you kick that woman?"

Kalani shrugged.

"Like I saw you take her food?" Liliha blurted. "How much did you steal from the supplies they landed today?"

"I take what's mine," Kalani answered.

"Then so will I."

Kalani grabbed her wrist in a strong grip. Liliha pried at Kalani's hand.

"Do you think you can do what you please? Do you think anyone cares what happens to you?" Kalani's voice was like a snake, cold and dangerous. "Do you think you're so pretty? So strong? I used to be pretty. I had long hair like yours. But I was smart enough to cut it off. Because I *am* strong. You? You'll be dead in a year."

Kalani twisted Liliha's arm until the skin burned and Liliha dropped the sack. Kalani gave it a solid kick; the sack billowed upward and disappeared into the darkness.

"You'd better think twice before you go stealing again," Kalani said, and thrust Liliha's arm away. She spat once on the ground, turned, and vanished into the night and the quickening rain.

Liliha scrambled in the direction she thought the sack had flown. The storm was upon Molokai with full force now. Her drenched hair fell in front of her face as she clambered onto her hands and knees and crawled through the mud to search for the sack. Mud oozed between her fingers; her knees sank into the streaming earth. An occasional sharp rock cut into her skin. The rain was penetrating and cold, aching deep into her bones. Liliha hunkered back onto her heels and squinted. She couldn't see any distance at all.

She didn't see Manukekua until he stood beside her. He stretched his hand toward Liliha. When she realized what he held, she stumbled to her feet.

"You found my sack!" she said, grabbing it from him and reaching inside to touch each item. She looked at him. "What are you doing out here?"

He didn't answer, just turned aside and gestured for her to come with him.

"Where?" Liliha called after him.

He walked on.

She thought that the compound lay in that direction, but she was so drenched and cold that she decided that maybe she *would* be willing to spend the night at the hospital if it came to that. She kept close behind Manukekua, who never stumbled over a rock or tangle of grass. They passed inside the fence, and Liliha saw that nothing remained of the fire but soaked ash. Near the cold remains, a few people lay curled into tight balls, their backs to the rain.

Manukekua passed the hospital.

"Where are we going?" Liliha asked. When he didn't answer, she stopped dead.

Manukekua turned around and retraced his steps. "The Captain's."

Liliha thought of the suffocating room, the darkness, the thud of the pewter mug slamming down on the table. She shook her head. "I don't want to go there."

"He's asleep now."

"He might wake up."

"He won't wake up. Believe me, he won't. He'll sleep till afternoon. There's space in the front room for you. But you'll have to leave in the morning, early. Just in case."

"I thought you said he'd sleep till afternoon," Liliha pointed out, but she followed him again, reluctantly. Manukekua took hold of the doorknob. Before he could push the door open, Liliha stopped him with a hand on his arm. "Manukekua. Why did you come after me? How did you know where I was?"

She saw how he glanced nervously at her hand and so she let go of his arm and clutched at her sack with both hands instead.

"I saw you leave, and I saw Kalani leave right after you. I had to go look for the Captain, but I thought you might be in trouble with the storm coming. And with Kalani out there."

"She tried to take this away from me." Liliha raised the sack.

"I was looking for you when I found that. When I saw what it was, I thought . . ." He shook his head.

"Thought what?" Liliha asked, her voice falling to a whisper as Manukekua opened the door.

He didn't answer, but slipped through the narrow gap and tugged Liliha after him. His stealth only made her more uneasy. It was so dark, so quiet inside.

But the quiet didn't last. Snores, enormous and thick, came from the back room. In moments of quiet between the Captain's snores, Liliha heard Manukekua moving around near her. He lit a candle on the table, and the flame sputtered whenever wind drove through chinks in the walls.

A woven mat lay unrolled in a corner of the room. Manukekua pointed at it. "You can sleep there," he whispered. He went into the back room and emerged with a blanket, which he set on the table.

"Is this where you usually sleep?" Liliha asked.

"I'll sleep in the back."

Liliha wondered if this was Manukekua's mat and whether there was another one in the back room or if he would sleep on the bare floor. Was this his blanket, too? He stood beside the table, watching her. The candlelight made the wound near his eye gleam silver, like the edge of a coin. He had the disease, the *ma'i pākē,* that was clear, but Liliha suddenly didn't care if he'd touched the same mat and blanket that she would use that night. She was just glad to be out of the rain and wind and was suddenly so exhausted that she could hardly keep to her feet. She gathered her hair to one side and twisted it. Drops of water scattered onto the floor.

Manukekua reached onto a shelf above the table and pulled down a plate with half a loaf of bread on it. He set the plate on the table and nodded at it.

"I'll wake you early," he whispered, backing clumsily from the room.

Liliha stared at the dark rectangle where he'd vanished and from which the Captain's snores still blasted. She picked up the candle and held it toward the shelf above the table. A knife gleamed near the edge of the shelf. Liliha put the candle back on the table and reached up to touch the knife. She nodded, running her fingertip along the blade, which was clean and sharp. The handle curved neatly into her palm.

She sawed at the bread until she'd cut away the heel. The Captain's snores had quieted. She imagined Manukekua in the dark silence. Maybe he was listening, his eyes open. Why was he willing to give her a place to spend the night and something to eat? What would happen to him if the Captain found out?

She devoured the heel of bread. Then, watching the doorway over her shoulder, she slid the knife into her sack. Maybe she could find a piece of wood and carve her own bowl from it, and a cup. It wasn't stealing, not really. The Captain should have given Liliha and the others bowls and cups as soon as they'd arrived on the peninsula.

And if the Captain finds the knife missing and blames Manukekua? She couldn't think about that.

She snuffed out the light and curled up on the mat.

At home, the lamp might still be burning. Uncle Malietoa would be in the single chair, of course, keeping it for himself. He'd be carving an oar or perhaps a toy canoe for barter with villagers who liked to give their children special treats. His carvings were expert, prized, and Liliha had learned some of his techniques by watching him furtively as he worked and practicing with his knife whenever she could filch it for a few minutes. Her mother would be sitting on the floor, legs crossed, a half-finished mat in her lap, her fingers weaving the brightly dyed leaves. Sudden pain twisted Liliha's face as she thought of her mother. It couldn't be possible that they would never see each other again. It couldn't!

The Captain began to snore again. Instead of keeping Liliha awake, the rhythmic noise put her into a sound sleep, unbroken until the next morning.

Liliha woke, confused, to the sight of Manukekua's stricken face as he pulled her from the mat.

His voice was a hiss. "He's waking up already. You can't stay. He'll be furious. He doesn't like natives coming in the house."

"And what are *you*?" she whispered, stumbling to her feet. Manukekua didn't answer, just thrust the sack at her and swept the bread crumbs from the table onto the floor. He didn't have to answer. She could see from the lightness of his skin, the roundness of his eyes, and the narrowness of his nose that he wasn't a full-blooded Hawaiian. One of his parents must been a *haole*.

When he snatched the front door open, abrupt sunlight blinded Liliha. Blue and cloudless, the sky held no trace of storm. Manukekua pointed past the fence. "If you go straight that way, you'll come to a hut. You'll know it when you see it. It looks more cared-for than the others. A woman named Pauahi lives there. I think she can help you. She'll make you work for it, but you'll have a place to stay."

"I don't need—"

Manukekua shook his head so hard that Liliha fell silent.

"It's better that way," he said. "For you to have someone to help you."

He glanced over his shoulder and stepped back into the house. The door swung neatly shut, leaving Liliha outside, alone.

CHAPTER SIX

LILIHA HAD NO TROUBLE FINDING PAUAHI'S HOME. SHE walked in the direction Manukekua had pointed until she came to a sturdy-looking hut with a well-cultivated garden around it. The dirt in front of the doorway had been swept clean of errant bits of grass. A woman sat in the doorway and knotted *kī* leaves together. She eyed Liliha.

"What are you making?" Liliha asked.

"Shoes. After I get the leaves braided."

Liliha looked down at Pauahi's feet. They were bare and swollen, the toes a half-dozen dark stubs.

"Not for myself," the woman said. "For barter."

"Barter? Who do you barter with?"

Pauahi nudged her chin toward the compound. "Everyone. I do good work. They come to me."

Liliha crouched beside her. "What do you trade for?"

The woman's shrewd eyes took in Liliha's damp dress and bedraggled sack. "You can look inside," she said. Liliha hesitated, then slowly rose and stepped through the doorway.

The room was dark, but once Liliha's eyes adjusted, she saw a pair of metal buckets by the door and pots brimming with utensils. A table with a single woven-back chair stood at one end of the room. At the other end, a pile of woven mats and blankets made an elaborate nest.

Liliha held her breath, imagining herself in possession of such wealth.

"You're new here, aren't you? You need a roof over your head," she heard Pauahi say, and she ducked outside again. "Sometimes," the woman continued in a speculative voice, "I barter for *help,* not for things. I trade, say, a place to sleep at night for a couple of buckets of fresh water."

"Where do you get fresh water?"

Pauahi pulled another knot snug. "You mean, where will *you* get fresh water." She looked up. "Wai'ale'ia Valley. That way. It's a hard walk for some."

"How hard?"

"That depends what state you're in." She jabbed a foot up into the air for Liliha to inspect. "It's maybe a couple of miles each way. It would take me the best part of a day to walk it. But then my feet are the part most afflicted. For you?" Sharp eyes examined Liliha's dusty feet. "Not too long. Half a morning. Less. Of course, it's toting the water back that's hard. Water's heavy. That's why I don't do it. I'd be dragging along all day."

Liliha hesitated. "So you trade with people to get them to go there for you?"

"Yes."

"Is it easy to find people to do that?"

Pauahi's eyes were bright as needles. "Very easy. People here have so little. *Most* people," she added with a smug curve to her mouth. "They're willing to carry water, oh, yes. The ones who have *kōkuas* to help them, they get by all right, but the others . . ." Shrugging, she pulled another knot tight.

Liliha leaned forward. "Why don't they—couldn't they just steal from you?"

Pauahi's mouth hardened with distaste. "They do, some of them. Opuhumanuu, that little rat, she sneaks around here and takes things from the garden. What she doesn't take, she's just as liable to trample on. That almost makes me madder than the stealing. And Kalani. I give her a present now and then and that takes care of things."

Liliha gaped. "You give presents to *her*?"

"To keep peace. A length of cloth or some breadfruit does wonders. But she respects me. People do. You have to let them know you're tough. I have a club and I've used it."

"And you respect her?"

"Hmm! Respect?" Pauahi shook her head. "But it's worth staying on good terms with anyone who's killed a man. If she could kill him, there's no reason she couldn't kill me. Or you."

"She's—she's what?"

Pauahi gave Liliha a keen gaze. "Now, you don't have anything to carry water in, do you?"

"No, but—do you mean that Kalani, she actually . . . ?" Liliha's throat tightened. Kalani was cruel, a bully, yes. But a murderer?

Pauahi ignored her stammering. "There are a couple of buckets inside the door. One of them is empty and the other's getting low. If you fill them, you can use some of the water." Pauahi held the braided cord straight out in front of her and pulled it taut, testing its strength. "You can use a fourth of the water in one of the buckets." She brought the cord back down to her lap.

Water. Liliha pushed away her fear of Kalani and tried to concentrate on what Pauahi had just proposed. She took a breath and said, "All the water in one of the buckets."

Pauahi peered at her. "What did you say, child?"

"I said I want all the water from one of the buckets. That only seems fair if I have to carry them all that way."

Pauahi's face clenched into an angry grimace. "Without the use of *my* buckets, you won't get any water at all."

Pauahi didn't like to be crossed, that was certain. The outrage that gripped her expression frightened Liliha, but she couldn't back down. If she did, Pauahi was sure to seize the advantage—and not just once, but over and over. The way Grandmother had. And Uncle Malietoa.

"Half," Pauahi said. "No more."

"A full bucket."

Pauahi pursed her lips. "That's ridiculous. No one has ever taken more than half. Those are *my* buckets."

"For all the good that does you, with feet like yours." Liliha waved a hand, casual and cruel, at Pauahi's feet, then looked away quickly.

Pauahi leaned inside the house and pulled out one of the buckets. "Down to here from the top," she said, slicing a line with the edge of her hand so that two thirds of the bucket was above the line and a third below. Liliha reluctantly nodded. "All right, then," Pauahi said.

Liliha picked up the buckets. When she hesitated, Pauahi

pointed southeast. "On the other side of the compound, you'll find a path. It goes through Wai'ale'ia Valley, all the way to the water. You'll see other people going there. Wai'ale'ia is where everyone gets fresh water. Be careful, though. Wai'ale'ia isn't always the safest place on Kalaupapa." Pauahi's eyes glinted as if the very idea of a safe place amused her. "They've had trouble with the valleys. Maybe people feel hidden there. That's where they make the beer and get drunk. I've heard about women there, too, attacked by men."

Liliha's stomach turned cold and sick.

Pauahi rolled her eyes. "Not much need for you to worry, young as you are. And you're hardly the prettiest girl in the world with that nose squat in the middle of your face like a squashed bug. It's a strange place, isn't it? It's better to be ugly than beautiful. Anyway, the middle of the day is the best time to go. There will be plenty of people after water. Don't let anyone take the buckets from you." A hint of worry etched Pauahi's forehead. Liliha was sure the concern was not for her, but for the threat to Pauahi's water supply. "So go on. Get the water."

Although the buckets banged against Liliha's legs as she walked, they weren't heavy and Liliha set them swinging forward and back as she passed the compound. She found the path on the far side, just as Pauahi had said she would. The path was narrow, the dirt hard-packed. Set back in the vegetation, occasional huts squatted like misshapen stumps. Liliha heard laughter, raucous and drunken, from inside one of them. She flinched and hurried past. Her eyes flickered from side to side, examining branches and leaves, imagining she saw movement behind them. Did Kalani have to fetch her own water? Liliha had no idea what she would do if she saw the woman striding along the path. She still wasn't sure she believed that Kalani had *killed* someone. Pauahi seemed like the type who loved gossip whether it was true or not.

She passed other people who traveled either direction along the path and was glad to see them even though she knew they wouldn't be much help if Kalani or anyone else attacked her. So many looked exhausted, lugging pails and awkward wooden tubs and old paint tins. When Liliha saw their feet, she wondered how they managed to walk such a distance at all. But then, what choice did they have?

She wondered if she would see Manukekua along this path. Surely he fetched water for the Captain just as Liliha was fetching water for Pauahi. The idea unsettled her. No, she wouldn't be like Manukekua. She wouldn't let herself be afraid of Pauahi. Manukekua *was* afraid of the Captain, wasn't he? Why else would he be so reluctant to cross him in even the smallest way? Why else did he stay cringing in that house? *Like you stayed hidden so long in Grandmother's house? Hardly coming out for days except to fetch meals?* She frowned and shook the thought from her head.

She could hear the stream now, water mumbling over rock, and she hurried forward until she saw it. A half-dozen lepers stooped down beside the water, trying to fill buckets and rotten tubs. Liliha averted her eyes and walked upstream several yards before she finally set the buckets down. She glanced at the lepers. A man held a bucket on its side, partly submerged, until it was nearly full; then he struggled to upright it again and to pull it free. A woman kneeling beside the water leaned forward until the ragged hem of her skirt trailed into the shallow stream. She cupped together her two ulcerated hands and scooped water into her mouth.

Liliha picked up one of Pauahi's pails and dragged it into the water, facing its open mouth into the flow. Then she pulled back on the handle until the bucket stood upright, its bottom resting precariously on the uneven stones of the stream bed. The bucket was nearly full. Liliha bent forward to grasp the handle. She tugged hard and managed to pull the bucket upward an inch or two before it settled back to the bottom of the stream again. She grabbed the handle and, rocking back, lugged the bucket out of the water and let it thud down onto the ground.

She managed to fill the other bucket in the same way. Gripping both handles, she took a few awkward steps. The weight seemed as if it would disjoint her shoulders and stretch her arms long and thin as cane. She had to stop frequently to shake her hands and fingers. It was exhausting and yet there were others, far worse off, who somehow managed to drag a single, sloshing container.

It took Liliha the better part of the morning to carry those buckets back to Pauahi's house. When she eased the buckets down onto the floor of the hut, water slopped over the rim of each. Liliha curled and straightened her arms until the pain eased.

Pauahi was inside now, lounging on a thick pile of sleeping mats. She sat up suddenly, then shuffled across the room.

"They aren't full," she observed.

"Close to it."

Pauahi bent down and tapped a finger against the metal. "This isn't full," she said. "Look at that." She pointed at the water level, which stood half the width of a hand below the rim.

Anger flashed through Liliha. Her arms still ached from the effort of carrying those buckets such a distance; deep red grooves cut across her fingers where she'd gripped the skinny handles.

"They're as full as I could get them," Liliha said. "Anyway, some water slopped out when I was carrying them back here. Do you know how *heavy* they are?"

"That isn't *my* concern." Pauahi drew a line across the bucket. "My share is the same. If you don't fill the bucket completely, it's your share that suffers, not mine."

"That isn't fair," Liliha burst out.

"We had a bargain," Pauahi calmly replied. "I drew the line, right there, and you agreed to it. That's the bargain."

Liliha was silent.

"Now." Pauahi shuffled to the doorway and peered out. "It's afternoon and I haven't eaten a thing since the sun came up." She went to a corner cluttered with calabashes and hollowed-out coconut shells, dried leaves and vines that could be used to weave mats or sandals or nets. Pauahi picked up a calabash and removed its clumsy lid. A dank odor of fish spread through the room. Pauahi pulled one out and wrapped several leaves around it. Carrying the package outside, she squatted beside an *imu,* an oven dug into the ground in front of the hut.

Liliha lowered herself to the floor. The muscles in her back and shoulders burned. She leaned gingerly against the wall, closed her eyes, and inhaled the smell. It made her think of the fish that Uncle Malietoa and the other men brought from the sea, and of the fish that Liliha used to catch—or pretend to catch—when she was very young and her father, still alive, took her out on the water.

She shook sudden tears from her eyes, jumped to her feet, and hurried outside. "Pauahi!"

The woman was squatting beside the oven, where the fish now cooked beneath hot stones.

"Pauahi, where did you get that fish?"

The woman shrugged. "From one of the others. I'm not sure I remember now exactly who." Her eyes glinted.

"And where did he get the fish? Did he trade for it? Did he catch it?"

"I'm sure I don't know." Pauahi shifted position, soured her mouth, and muttered, "I paid too much for it, though, I can tell you that."

"Is there a good fishing spot on Kalaupapa?"

"Oh, no. Only bad ones. Maybe if you could get far enough out in a boat, it would be better, but when you're wading close to shore—and the surf's too rough to go out very far at all—you don't catch much. That's why the bastard was able to drive such a mean bargain."

Liliha pictured Kalaupapa's rough shores and rocky surf. Even if she had a canoe, she wouldn't be able to pull out easily into that surf to fish. But what if she could wade out with a net? A broad net, with a small enough weave that even little fish would find escape impossible? Or a net made like a sack, open at one end? And if someone else would go with her, together they would be able to use a much bigger net, each person holding one side of it. Maybe Manukekua? Or Hana, if Liliha could find her again. The aroma rising from the oven was savory and sharp and whetted Liliha's hunger. She'd eaten nothing since the night before when Manukekua had given her the bread.

"I need a net," Liliha said.

Pauahi's gaze sharpened. "Why?"

"To catch fish."

"It's not like home, you know. It's not so easy here."

"Do you have a net, Pauahi?"

"I might."

Liliha bit at her tongue, then reluctantly said, "Of course, I'd give you part of what I catch."

"Half." Pauahi stood and went inside. When she reappeared, she carried a folded net, which she handed to Liliha. "Half. Don't pretend to forget and don't try to cheat me."

Liliha nodded, shaking the net open. It was smaller than she'd hoped and the weave was too large and loose. She looked up questioningly at Pauahi, who snapped, "That's the only one I've got right now."

Pauahi crouched beside the oven again. The scent of fish was only making Liliha aware of her empty stomach, so she gathered up the net and started toward the ocean.

"It won't be easy," Pauahi called after her.

Liliha walked the half mile to the ocean. At the shore, she

looked down, not only to avoid stepping on anything sharp, but also to watch for the remains of any fish that might have washed ashore. She saw a few splinters of bone, an occasional tiny, tattered head. Nothing that promised a good catch.

The waves spilling over her feet were fast and rough. Liliha pushed out deeper into the water until it buried her to her chest. Water churned around her skirt, threatening to drag her farther out. The sodden cloth hung like an anchor from her waist. She should have taken the skirt off and she would have, if only . . . she glanced back toward shore. There was no telling who might come walking along and see her. She remembered what Pauahi had said about some of the men attacking women and felt her stomach turn over.

Liliha turned back to face the sea. At the horizon, the water appeared calm, almost motionless, but here the waves slapped at her arms and spray burst into her face, blinding her. The water made her shiver. What had the Scottish doctor told her? An insistent chill deep in the bones was one of the effects of leprosy. Shaking the thought from her head, Liliha stiffened her muscles to stop their trembling.

She grasped opposite edges of the net and, sinking down into the water, swept the net in an arc in front of her. At home, the *mahimahi* and *manini* were so plentiful that such a simple technique would sometimes meet with success. Children were sent out with similar nets, the fish they caught added to the haul brought back by the men in their canoes. Here, though, Liliha dragged the net up to the surface again and again, only to find it empty.

She waded farther out and stood on tiptoe, the water closing over her shoulders. A huge boulder jagged up nearby, waves smashing against it.

She scrambled onto the rock, scraping her knees as she climbed. The rock was slippery with foam. Crouched at one edge, her hands gripping the stone, Liliha peered down at the water. It was so rough that she couldn't see to the bottom the way she could at home. Here, she couldn't see more than a handspan beneath the surface. She waited, watching for the quick glimmer that indicated a school of fish. At home, the wait was never long and the frequent appearance of bright pink and blue and scarlet fish made the time pass quickly. At home, her favorite fish, the beautiful *aholeahole,* would delight her by sometimes glinting into view. At Kalaupapa, unfortunately, no spectacular creatures interrupted the boredom.

Although she was patient and alert, by late afternoon she'd caught only two small fish, one that she couldn't identify and another that looked somewhat like an *ahi,* except that she'd never seen one so small. The *ahi* fishermen pulled onto their canoes could be immense. There was part of a purple-blue tentacle caught in the net as well. Nothing else. She squatted on the beach. Her skirt clung to her legs like seaweed, dank and cold. The fish lay, side-by-side, in front of her. She shook her head. Neither fish was even as big as her hand.

It was so different here. So hard. At home, huge marlin glided in the depths until the men captured them and hauled them back to the village in triumph. The fish here looked as paltry and ravaged as the lepers.

For a moment she thought about hiding these fish, burying them somewhere along the shore and going to Pauahi with empty hands. Pauahi didn't deserve half of *anything*.

But it was Pauahi's net. No matter how loosely woven or almost useless.

I saw you steal, Kalani's voice hissed in her head.

The *taro* first. Then the knife. And the fish?

"What was I supposed to do?" Liliha muttered. "Starve?" Anyway, why should it matter what people thought of her here? And as for Kalani calling her a thief—well, Kalani was a thief herself and maybe something a lot worse.

As she glanced at her catch, Liliha suddenly laughed, imagining Pauahi's face when she saw the single measly fish that was her portion. Liliha laughed harder, her shoulders hunching forward. Pauahi was getting just what she deserved.

But Pauahi didn't seem at all surprised when Liliha smacked the unidentifiable fish onto the table in front of her. "I said it wouldn't be easy," she remarked, working a scale loose with one twisted fingernail. "Someone who didn't know Kalaupapa might think you'd hidden a huge stash somewhere; lucky for you, I know how bad the catch is here. You're wasting your time." Still, no matter how much disdain Pauahi might have felt for the single fish staring up at her with one flat, round eye, she tucked it carefully into a calabash in the corner.

"Never let anything go to waste," she advised, her gaze sliding to Liliha. "Not here."

Liliha changed into her other skirt and blouse. The dry cloth felt good against her skin. She took out her knife, sliced the head from the fish that reminded her of an *ahi,* and slit the body open. When she set the knife down on the table, the quiet in the room intensified. Liliha looked up to see Pauahi staring at the knife and curved her hand protectively around the handle.

"Is that yours?" Pauahi said.

Liliha's stomach revolved in a slow circle. Sweat sprouted from the palms of her hands. "Yes."

"You brought it with you?"

"My mother gave me a sack of things to bring with me, things she thought I would need."

"A knife like that?" Pauahi nodded approvingly. "Your mother must be very practical. You wouldn't believe the useless trash people drag here with them."

Liliha returned to cleaning the fish. She felt the pressure of Pauahi's stare, then the woman snorted, hobbled to the door, and went outside, ducking her head back through the doorway long enough to say, "If you'll clean my fish, too, you can use the oven out here to cook them both."

Liliha removed the most obvious bones and thought about her mother. Maybe her mother *hadn't* chosen the most practical things, but she'd given Liliha the things that had mattered to her. Things she'd thought Liliha would cherish. Liliha bit the inside of her cheek, but the physical pain couldn't take away the pain of loneliness.

Liliha ate carefully, taking small bites, which she chewed at the front of her mouth, using her tongue to ferret out the tiny slivers of bone. She spat the slivers onto the ground beside her. Pauahi did the same.

"I can't say you cleaned this very well," Pauahi said, and spat again, directly onto the hot stones they'd used to cook the fish. Liliha heard the saliva's quick sizzle.

"The fish are too small. I couldn't see all the bones."

If Pauahi answered, Liliha didn't hear. Movement caught at the corner of her eye and she turned to stare after it. In the distance she saw the Captain hurrying *makai,* heading the same direction she'd taken earlier to the sea. He was a dark silhouette moving against a sky smeared orange with sunset. Manukekua followed right behind.

Squinting against the light, Liliha watched until they both disappeared. She swung around to face Pauahi. "Why is he going that way? That's where I went to fish."

Pauahi scratched at her scalp. "The only thing that direction is the ocean."

"In that great coat of his . . . ?" Liliha said wonderingly.

"Well, he'd hardly be getting *into* the water. I hear . . ."

Her palms pressed together, Liliha leaned toward Pauahi. "What do you hear?"

Pauahi's eyes narrowed. "I wonder that it matters to you."

"I hate him." When Pauahi didn't answer, Liliha added, "He refused to give us any food, any shelter, any help at all."

Pauahi snorted with laughter. "He's never been worth a damn. None of them is any good. You're a fool if you expect otherwise."

Liliha lowered her head and muttered, "We were all fools then, weren't we?"

Pauahi's eyes glittered. "*I* wasn't. I knew better than to expect some sort of paradise. But it seems like I was about the only one who didn't come here with all kinds of grand ideas."

"Food? A place to live? Those are grand ideas?"

"In this place, yes. And the sooner people get over their foolishness, the better." Pauahi chewed the last bit of fish and licked the oil from her hands. "I hear he's crazy. The Captain."

"Crazy?"

"No one's sure what happened to him. There's always been something off about him. I've heard some say he's crazy with missing the sea. With sailing."

"Then why doesn't he hire onto a ship?"

Pauahi raised her eyebrows. "Maybe he can't stand the thought of being part of a crew, not being in command."

"But if he was a ship's captain before, why couldn't he be a captain again?"

"That's the question, isn't it? No one knows, though I heard someone say something once about a war in the United States. That something bad happened to him there. But I don't know any more than that."

"And the boy who's with him? Manukekua. That's not his son, is it?"

Pauahi seemed to find that hilarious. "Son? More like his servant. *Haoles* are lazy. They want lots of servants waiting on them."

"But how did—?"

Pauahi shook her head and pulled herself to her feet. "I'm tired. And hungry. I'm going inside to eat the rest of my *poi* and then I'm going to sleep. Clean up the bones before I step on one and get it in my foot. When you're done, you can sleep in the corner across from me. The mats are mine, though. Don't touch them." Pauahi limped inside.

Haoles weren't the only ones who wanted to be waited on, Liliha thought, picking fragments of bone out of the dirt. Her arms ached when she thought about the buckets just inside the door. How many days would it be before Pauahi would want her to fetch more water?

And if I don't, I'll be living outside.

Outside didn't seem so terrible on a clear, warm night. But when storms hit . . . She shivered, remembering the fury of rain and wind. She and Manukekua were alike. Both slaves for shelter. She stopped just outside the doorway to Pauahi's hut and stared at it. If Kalaupapa peninsula was a prison, then this hut seemed like a cell deep within that prison. She would stay with Pauahi only as long as she absolutely had to.

Liliha closed her eyes as she stepped inside.

Escape from Pauahi's. And then? Was it possible? Did anyone ever escape from Kalaupapa?

CHAPTER SEVEN

DURING THE NEXT FEW WEEKS, LILIHA SETTLED INTO A routine of sorts. Early each morning she took the net to fish. She'd bartered her labor for some of Pauahi's *kī* leaf cords and used them to tighten the weave of the net. But the alterations didn't do much to improve the quality of the fish she caught. She tried different spots along the shore, all equally poor, yielding nothing but an occasional *manini* or a strangely stunted *ulua.* She fetched leaves from *kī* plants, which she and Pauahi then used to weave mats. She tended the garden, pulling out weeds, and making sure the fledgling sweet potato plants looked healthy. Every third day she toted water from Wai'ale'ia.

She worked hard each day, but when she tried to bargain for better payment from Pauahi, the woman said, "We've set our bargain, and if you don't like it, you can go starve out there by yourself. Go ahead."

Liliha wasn't starving, quite, but she was hungry all the time. The fish she caught and the pittance of *poi* and sweet potato that Pauahi grudgingly paid her were never enough to fill her stomach. Each meal she ate only brought her stomach awake, growling and churning. Almost a month, and no boats had arrived with more rations.

Pauahi let her leave to fish and fetch water, but otherwise wanted her to stay near the hut in case she needed Liliha's help. When Liliha passed the compound on her way to the stream, she always stopped to look for Hana and Ahia, but she never saw them. She thought she glimpsed Manukekua once, but he slipped inside the Captain's house so quickly that she didn't have a chance to call out to him. She also looked for the little boy she'd seen crouching by the fence that first day, and rested easier when she saw him nestled against an older woman, both of them eating something from the same bowl. The woman was grotesque, nearly as deformed and emaciated as the patients in the hospital, but the boy seemed content to be with her.

In the evenings, when she had time and sufficient daylight, she brought out the knife and driftwood she'd found along the shore on her way to fish and began to carve. The pieces of wood were small and usually in bad shape, half rotted or deformed with knots, but Liliha still turned her skill on them. She made a bowl first, shallow and broad across the top, and then a cup. She worked much more slowly than Uncle Malietoa would have, but with equal concentration. The curves of the wood calmed her as she smoothed the surfaces. The cup was even, balanced, with a pleasing shape. When she sat outside in the twilight, peeling away layers of wood, she could pretend she was back home, her mother working nearby, Grandmother asleep, and Uncle Malietoa blessedly away, drinking and gossiping with the other men of the village or repairing his boat.

One morning, she put a finished cup and plate and a pair of spoons in her sack and started for the door just after dawn, carrying the sack instead of the usual net.

Pauahi snapped up from her nest of mats. "Aren't you going fishing?"

"No."

"Why not?" Pauahi's gaze flicked toward the sack. "You really think people will trade you anything of value for a bowl or a spoon?"

"Yes."

Liliha stooped to pass through the doorway when Pauahi called out, "Wait." Liliha hesitated, then slowly turned. "Those things you carved. You were sitting right there in front of my hut when you made them. If I weren't giving you a place to live and food to eat, you'd never have been able to carve *anything*."

"Are you saying you want part of whatever I trade them for?"

The rising sun cut across the room, casting Pauahi's face into sharp blocks of light and dark. "*If* you trade them." Her eyes glittered acquisitively. "It's only fair."

"No." Liliha ducked outside. From behind her came an outraged squawk.

Liliha didn't look back.

At the compound, she crouched by the *pū hala* tree and began to lay out her few wares. Sunlight splintered through the branches overhead; she'd rubbed and polished the plate and cup so vigorously that they gleamed wherever the sun struck them. The curve of each spoon might have been the graceful back of a dolphin leaping into view, glistening with water.

Early in the morning, the square was nearly empty except for a few men and women who slept in front of the hospital or alongside the compound fence.

Gradually others began to gather. Some came from outside the compound and some emerged from the hospital. The last were *kōkuas,* Liliha guessed. Several lepers squatted outside the Captain's door, as if they expected him to appear and throw alms to them. Liliha gave them a scornful glance. They were going to have a long wait. Others meandered around the square, then sank to the ground and did nothing at all. She recognized a noisy group beside the hospital. There were the card players she'd seen at the bonfire that first night. A couple of men from Liliha's transport sat with them. The cards were out again and there was a moment of silence as, one by one, the players showed their hands. Then violent cursing erupted and one of the losers shoved another man. The shouting faded to a resentful murmur as the dealer swiftly shuffled and tossed cards down for the next round.

She tried to meet the eyes of each person who walked by, but no one came to look at her carvings. She pushed the cup farther into the sunlight. No one even glanced at it. How was she supposed to attract attention?

Jumping up, Liliha paced out from under the tree and waved one arm grandly toward the plate. "Who wants to strike a bargain?" she called. "A cup, a plate, a spoon?"

Heads turned, bodies shifted. People stared at her without

answering. The gamblers had things to trade, but they turned back to their game.

Liliha squatted beside the tree again. Her hands ground together. Was Pauahi right? No one wanted the things she'd carved. She might as well have spent those hours fishing instead. At least she might have caught *something* more to help fill out her meager diet.

"Liliha!"

She raised her head.

"Liliha." Hana broke into an enormous smile as she rolled across the compound. She pulled Liliha up into a generous hug. "Where have you been, child? I asked around, but no one recognized you or knew where you were. I was worried about you. The storm that first night!"

Liliha couldn't help smiling. "I was worried about *you* that night, Hana. How are you?"

"I'm all right, but Ahia . . ." Hana's face sobered. "He gets fevers. Sometimes he's not too bad, but sometimes he's very sick."

"But where do you live?"

Hana drew closer and bent her head down. "We've been at Kalaupapa landing."

"Where we came on shore?" Liliha said doubtfully. "You really did go back there?"

"Ahia insisted. He was hoping for rations, you know, and even after we got there and found all the rations gone, he thought there might soon be another boat. He said that if we explained there was a mistake, told the crew about people we know in Honolulu . . ." She shook her head; a shadow caught her face, then disappeared. "But no boat came, of course."

"And you were trapped by the storm."

"Oh, no. No, we rode out the storm comfortably enough except that I was worried about you. A woman named Martha took us in." She smiled at Liliha's confusion. "Do you remember the houses, not too far down the beach from where we landed?"

"Are the people who live there . . . ?" Liliha broke off.

"Lepers? No. *Kama'āina*. Native born. They've always lived there and they aren't about to leave, no matter what the government wants them to do." She leaned toward Liliha. "There are good Christians among them. A minister from a mission on another part of the island comes over the *pali* when he can."

"Over the *pali*?" Liliha's head snapped up. "People do that?"

"Not many. But, yes, a few. I haven't seen any myself, except the minister, but Martha told me that visitors come every once in a while. A father came just a couple of months ago to see his son who has leprosy. He stayed in one of the other houses at Kalaupapa."

"But . . . but I thought no one was allowed to visit."

Hana nodded. "Well, whatever the rules, visitors *do* come. And the people at Kalaupapa can sometimes give them a place to stay for a short time. I don't know what would happen if the government decided to send in inspectors and crack down on it."

She said something else, but Liliha didn't hear. Her head felt like it had split open and the whole world rushed into it. She could barely breathe. If she could just let her mother know, somehow . . . But how would her mother ever get to Kalaupapa? The boats wouldn't bring her in if she wasn't one of the sick or a *kōkua*. And if she landed on the southern part of Molokai, she'd have to come down the *pali*. Liliha turned to look south. The cliff was steep, almost vertical, but if the minister and other visitors could handle the descent, so could her mother. And if her mother could just see what this place was really like, she'd do anything to help Liliha. Maybe even help her to escape.

"Do people ever leave?" Liliha asked.

"Well, the visitors don't stay forever. And some of the *kama'āina* go to other villages over the *pali*. And the minister, of course." Hana thought a moment. "Martha even sends letters along with the minister. He gets them to her sister somehow."

"What about lepers?"

"Lepers?"

"Do they ever leave?"

Understanding flashed on Hana's face. "No."

Liliha's voice shook with urgency. "Are you *sure*?"

Hana stood back, watched Liliha. Her eyes were sad. "No, I'm not sure. But I haven't heard of any lepers leaving. And, Liliha, leaving wouldn't be a good idea."

"Why not?"

"Where would you—where would a leper go? Where people wouldn't recognize what he was and turn him in? Always hiding, always hunted—no, it's better to stay among your own people."

These aren't my people, Liliha wanted to yell. How could Hana be so blind, so accepting?

"Liliha."

Liliha blinked up at Hana. Hana bent down and grasped her

wrist with one hand as if measuring the circumference of flesh, the diameter of bone. "You look thin. Are you getting enough to eat?"

Liliha paused. She was hungry all the time, but it was impossible to think of that now when her head was filled with pictures of her mother traveling to Molokai, visiting Liliha in one of the houses at Kalaupapa landing. Maybe Martha's house, where Hana lived. Surely they'd let her mother stay for a few days.

"Liliha?"

"I'm all right."

"Are you sure?"

"I'm sure."

Hana clasped Liliha's hands with fingers that were warm and plump and callused at the tips. Liliha's mother had calluses like that, little plateaus of flesh as hard and flat as coins. "But where are *you* living?"

When Liliha explained about her arrangement with Pauahi, Hana frowned. "I don't like the sound of it, Liliha. It's not good for you to be with someone who can't see past the work she can get out of you." Something about Liliha's expression must have alarmed her, because Hana suddenly patted her shoulder and smiled. "Still, I'm glad you have a place to stay. I was so worried. Do you know that one of the women who came here with us died? I found her in *there* one morning." Hana nodded toward the hospital. "She was still alive, but very far gone. She'd been living outside, no shelter, no food, and a man—" Hana caught herself. "Oh, I *am* glad you have somewhere to live!"

Liliha burst out: "What if I came to Kalaupapa? To live there, too?"

Hana looked stricken; her face paled. "Oh, Liliha, I *can't* offer you a place in Martha's house."

"Is it because you're Christian? Is that why they help you?"

"They live by the Word, yes, but I think it's because of the minister who visits from over the *pali*. It turns out that I knew his sister in Honolulu. We were friends, as a matter of fact. I think that's why they've made an exception for us. Please try to understand, Liliha. It's Martha's house, not mine, not Ahia's. We're really just guests there ourselves. And even that isn't something I want most people to know. Lepers aren't supposed to mingle with the *kama'āina*."

"But they'll break the rules for you because you're one of them."

"Liliha, please try to understand."

But Liliha didn't understand. Weren't the missionaries always going on about love and doing good deeds and helping others?

"They've told me there are other Christians here," Hana said gently. "Right here at Kalawao, among the sick. They call themselves Siloama. The Church of the Healing Spring. Although there isn't an actual church yet. But they might be a comfort."

Liliha retreated beneath the *pū hala* tree again. Those Siloama people weren't going to be any help to her, she could tell Hana that right now.

With a low sigh, Hana squatted and, picking up the cup, ran her fingers along its satin rim. "You made this?"

"Yes."

Hana turned the cup around and around. "Such a peaceful shape you've given it. I'm glad you're able to think of peaceful things."

Liliha shrugged. "I just carved. I wasn't really thinking of anything."

"No?"

Liliha shook her head, stared at the ground. She wouldn't tell Hana how she'd imagined being at home beside her mother while she'd carved these. Hana would worry that she was thinking about escape. Frustration made a hard knot in Liliha's gut. She was determined to get word to her mother, to bring her mother here and, with her mother's help, to escape and live . . . well, it hardly mattered where. Maybe near home. She didn't even care if she had to stay in hiding.

But *how* was she going to arrange all this? How was she going to tell her mother anything? Hana would know what to do. Hana was so capable, so practical, and she'd lived among the *haoles* for so long. She knew their ways. Hana was the one person she knew could help her, but she suspected that Hana *wouldn't* help. Not if the goal was to escape. She'd expect Liliha to stay here among "her people." It wasn't fair.

Liliha glanced up. Hana was watching her with an anxious face.

"So," Liliha finally said, touching the plate. "Do you know anyone who might want to buy these?"

Hana inclined her head toward the hospital. "They might not be able to buy, but they could use a cup, a spoon. It would be a help."

Liliha looked over Hana's shoulder at the hospital. The door stood firmly shut; sun glared off the windows, making them opaque. "Do you go in there a lot?" she asked.

"On occasion."

"Why?"

"There's a sorry need for nurses."

Liliha cocked her head to one side, puzzling. "Were you a nurse back in Honolulu?"

"I tried to help. You should come into the hospital with me." Liliha remembered the bottles, the murky light, and—worst of all—the stench. "I can't," she said in a rush. "Not today. I have these things to sell."

Hana nodded. "Even a spoon would be a blessing to them, Liliha."

Liliha looked at the ground, then at the sky blazing blue past the hospital roof. "I made them to sell."

She could feel Hana's gaze settle on her. When Liliha finally met Hana's eyes, they held no anger, no disdain. "Of course," Hana said simply. She glanced toward the hospital. "I should go in. It's so good to see you, Liliha. Come see me, will you?"

"At Kalaupapa?"

Hana nodded.

"Even if it's against the rules?" Faint bitterness tinged Liliha's words.

"I don't think anyone will care if you just visit for a while." Hana took the cup. "So, what would you want for this? Would part of a loaf of bread be enough?" Hana opened the sack she'd carried with her from the other side of the peninsula that morning. "It's good," she said, pulling out a hunk of bread, which she put in Liliha's hands. "Martha made it. I'd like to offer you the whole loaf, but I need some for the sick. If it isn't enough . . ."

The bread was crusty and dark, heavy as a stone. Liliha bent over it and breathed. The aroma made her dizzy.

"The minister brought flour with him the last time he came over," Hana said.

Liliha gawked up at the cliff again.

"All right, then," Hana said gently. "Will you be here tomorrow morning, too?" Liliha managed to look away from the *pali*. "Then I'll see you tomorrow. I'm glad of that." She patted Liliha's shoulder. A moment later, Hana was at the hospital, trying to pull the door open while clutching her sack and the cup.

Liliha tore the heel from the bread and stuffed piece after piece into her mouth, swallowing hard. She ate half of the food before she was able to stop herself. Then she shoved the remaining chunk into her sack and pulled the drawstring. She didn't intend to let Pauahi near it.

Her thoughts tumbled. If Hana didn't approve of escape and couldn't be trusted to help her, then how was she ever going to get word to her mother? How would her mother get here?

Liliha picked up the plate and spoons and stepped away from the tree. She *would* find someone to trade with and she'd keep every last bit of food or scrap of cloth she earned for herself. How ridiculous of Pauahi to imagine she deserved any of it! If only Liliha could find an abandoned hut that hadn't completely fallen down or already been claimed or . . . or build her own and be free of Pauahi entirely.

And have a place where her mother could stay. Then there

would be no need for her mother to stay with Hana or any of those people at Kalaupapa landing.

She nodded with sharp decision.

She *would* have her own hut, and soon. She would get away from Pauahi, get away from all of them. And somehow, Hana or no Hana, she'd find a way to get a message to her mother. There *had* to be a way.

She held the plate out in front of her, waved the spoons, and stepped up to a man. It was midmorning now, the sun bright, and the man squinted up at her.

"You need a spoon, don't you?" she said. "What will you give me for it?" He stared at her with stupefied eyes. "What do you have left from your last rations?"

His fingers fluttered against his legs. "Some salt beef. Not much."

"How much?"

He stared at her as if she frightened him. "How much?" she insisted. He shook his head. *"How much?"* He raised a hand in front of his face and turned away.

He stayed in that position, not speaking, not looking at her, even after she stepped away and headed to a knot of women gathered near the road. One of the women cast a sullen look at Liliha, but the others peered at her with curiosity.

She held the spoons toward them like flowers. "Beautiful." She said the word in a slow, savoring voice. "Do you see how beautiful?" The wood glowed in the sunlight.

A woman stared at her face. "You were on the boat with me," the woman said.

"I was?" Liliha didn't recognize her, but then the woman

was already bony and threadbare, her gaunt face grimy and her hair twisted in oily clumps. Liliha wondered for a moment if she looked like that, too, then she turned her attention to one of the spoons again. "Isn't it smooth? See it shine?"

Another woman reached out, her crabbed fingers struggling open.

"Beautiful," the woman whispered, touching the spoon. A line deepened across her forehead. "What does it cost?"

"What do you have?"

Liliha didn't leave the compound until midafternoon, but when she did, a thick piece of salted beef, a small bag of rice, a chunk of salted salmon, and the remainder of Hana's bread swung in her sack. As she cut toward Pauahi's house, her gaze swept the ground, searching for any piece of wood or planking, however small, that she could add to her inadequate stockpile.

She stopped once, turned back to look at the *pali* towering into the sky. She wondered how hard the climb would be and what lay on the other side. Liliha's hands clenched. She'd find a way to bring her mother here, a way to get down the *pali* if it came to that. And then . . .

Then her mother would help her escape.

With sudden energy, she ran until she reached Pauahi's hut. As she ducked inside, Pauahi was already staring at her with greedy eyes. Without a word, Liliha flung herself down, yanked the bread out of the sack, and ate. Pauahi opened her mouth to speak, but closed it when Liliha shook her head and pounded the bread back into the sack.

"No, Pauahi. It's mine. Not yours."

The knife Liliha wore tucked under the waist of her skirt

pressed against her skin. The blade was warm. It gave her strength.

"Mine," she said. Energy surged through her again. At that moment she could have knocked down the walls if she wanted to, run with a hundred full buckets from Wai'ale'ia.

"Mine."

CHAPTER EIGHT

THE NEXT MORNING THE AIR HUNG SULTRY AND WET across Molokai and the ocean was warm as blood. Liliha had been fishing since dawn, her arms moving the net mechanically, her attention focused on the problem of how to contact her mother. She looked up from her work, pulling one arm out of the water and dragging it across her forehead to wipe away sweat. She froze in that position; her gaze locked on the horizon and the long, dark shape sliding across the water. At the same instant, she heard the shrill whistle. A ship! For weeks she'd been waiting for another boat to appear. Shipments were supposed to come more frequently than that, but as Pauahi had noted: "Those government people. What do they care if the food comes on time? You can bet they're feasting!"

Liliha snatched the fishing net out of the water, muttering at the weight of the wet fibers, and slogged impatiently toward land. When she reached shore, she roughly folded the net and, gripping it hard with one hand, ran in the direction of Kalaupapa landing. By the time she got there, her throat was raw and a cramp pinched her side.

A pair of rowboats had landed, provisions dumped beside them on the beach, and lepers already were struggling over the food. A sailor guided a third boat toward shore. He was completely bald, and the sun blazed white against his scalp. A half-dozen people crouched in his boat. Behind the sailor swayed a stack of crates.

When the boat lunged onto the sand, Liliha was there to meet it. She glanced behind her. How long before Kalani appeared? Liliha's heart lurched. The bald sailor had barely stepped onto land before Liliha shoved past him and the new arrivals. She reached for the first crate and tugged at it. The weight surprised her. Grunting, she started to lift the crate, but the sailor pushed her hand away from it and swung it onto the beach. The wood creaked, settling into the sand.

Other lepers pushed up behind Liliha as she crouched beside the crate and pried at the top slats with her fingers until she thought her bones would break. A splinter slid into one fingertip. Wincing, Liliha bit at the splinter with her teeth, pulled it out, and spat it onto the ground.

Nails shrieked as the first slat came loose. She tossed the board aside and wormed her hand inside the crate. She pulled out a bundle of *pa'i 'ai,* then another and another, until they made a squat tower beside her. She glanced over her shoulder. A man was tearing open another crate, this one filled with dried salmon, tough strips of flesh tied together in makeshift packages with string.

Liliha could remember Pauahi's words precisely, could see the older woman ticking off the list on her knotty fingers: "Each person is supposed to get three pounds of beef or salmon and a bundle of *pa'i 'ai* or rice every week. That's how it's *supposed* to work. Not that a boat comes every week. And when they do come late, they don't necessarily bring extra food to make up for the rations we've missed. There's plenty of people trying to grab more than their share and plenty of other people losing out." Pauahi had finished with a sneer for the losers.

Liliha took two bricks of *pa'i 'ai*—one for herself and one for Pauahi—then whirled around and pushed toward the other crate, where she snatched up two bundles of salmon. Better salmon than the beef, which was so tough, it was hard to chew and so salty that it burned the mouth.

She hunched off to one side and spread the net on the sand. After she dropped the rations onto the center of the net, she pulled the edges together to form a makeshift sack and flung it over her shoulder.

She stopped short when she saw someone familiar wander past, moving vaguely toward the other two boats and the piles of supplies beside them, which were already being ravaged.

"Ahia!" Liliha called, hurrying to him. But Ahia stumbled back until he and Liliha stood four or five paces apart, staring at each other. Ahia was even thinner now.

He looked past her and began to shuffle forward, his bony shoulders slumped.

"Ahia!" He didn't look back. He trailed across the rocky shore toward a heap of crates. A growing mob of lepers boiled around the boxes and, in the center of the mob, Liliha saw Kalani raise a heavy, gnarled stick overhead. The club smashed down, but the mob churning around Kalani was so chaotic that Liliha couldn't see the victim. Opuhumanuu stood beside Kalani along with the man who'd been with them the morning Liliha first arrived at Kalaupapa. The man was gathering rations onto a wooden handcart. Kalani drove the club into the shoulder of a woman who tried to take something from the cart.

At the next pile of supplies farther down shore, a fight broke out. Two men cursed at each other, shouting, so Liliha could hear every word they said, and lunged at each other with their fists.

The wagon Liliha had seen that first day trundled along the beach and stopped. As more lepers arrived at the landing site, the chaos increased. Liliha stared for a moment. How many people were there? Two hundred? Three hundred? And how many more were too sick to walk to Kalaupapa? Some of the lepers were shouting and shoving. Others were too weak to do more than limp around the supplies and crawl across broken wooden slats.

The slats! Liliha was furious at herself. Why hadn't she taken any of those boards to carve later? They'd be too thin to use for a cup or a bowl, but she might get spoons and combs from them.

Just looking at the angry crowd festering around the crates made Liliha's heart thud. She didn't want to go near them, but she had to. Wood was hard to come by and she couldn't afford to leave behind whatever scraps she could get. As she edged into the mob, she saw the bald sailor dump the last of the *pa'i 'ai* out of a crate and heave the crate into the boat. He was strong and the emptied containers were light. Liliha watched helplessly as he tossed crate after crate, board after board, into the boat and set off rowing for the ship.

She turned toward the heap of supplies where Kalani was distributing—and denying—rations. A withered man, clutching a tiny package to his chest, skittered out of the mob and, in the instant before the crowd closed behind him, Liliha could see a wreckage of wood scattered on the ground.

Did she dare? Her pulse stabbed at her throat.

Was she going to let Kalani scare her away from a good stock of wood? She watched how people cowered and scurried under the threat of Kalani's club and her vicious yell. There were a few others like Kalani, ferocious, some armed with sticks and one woman who held a glinting knife in her hand; they worked swiftly, looting the supplies, watching Kalani warily even as Kalani kept a distance and glared fury at them.

Liliha forced herself to walk forward; fear clung to her as stubbornly as barnacles on the hull of a boat.

She hunched over, making herself small, and slipped sideways through the crowd. Confusion engulfed her; rasping cries, jabbering pleas, wavering arms, staggering legs. Liliha set her net down at her feet and crouched to snatch up a long, splintered board. Wet sand speckled one side of the board. A pair of nails stabbed out from the far end like long fangs.

She heard Kalani give a triumphant cry.

Still crouching, Liliha looked up and froze. Kalani loomed above her, face dark against the sky. Kalani seemed like a giant, her club raised high above her head.

Liliha realized that Kalani wasn't shrieking at her, but at someone else collapsed nearby on the ground. Liliha leaned forward, her knees pressing hard into grit. She saw a stained white shirt with limp cuffs, a wilted collar gray with sweat, delicate hands curled against the sand. The man turned his face to one side. Ahia.

Liliha glanced around wildly. Where was Hana? If she was nearby, the surging, squabbling crowd concealed her.

Kalani brought the club smashing down. But instead of striking Ahia, the club cracked against the board Liliha swung protectively above him. At the impact, splinters tore through Liliha's hand. Tears sprang from her eyes, but she didn't let go of the board. She glanced up, expecting Kalani to smash the club down again at any second. Kalani held the club up close to her face and squinted at it in dismay. A long, deep fissure nearly split the club in two.

"Ahia," Liliha murmured, grasping his hand. It was feverish despite the cool sand that crusted his skin. His fingers were limp and wet as seaweed. Liliha had to grip them hard to keep them from slipping out of her own hand. "Ahia!" His eyes turned toward her in confusion. "Ahia! Get up!" She tugged at him and tried to watch both Kalani and the net near her feet.

Kalani tossed the fractured club to one side, not glancing to see if it hit anyone; her eyes fixed on Liliha.

"How long does it take for you learn?" she snapped.

"He hasn't done anything," Liliha said, her eyes cutting toward Ahia.

"A thief *would* speak for a thief."

"Ahia isn't—"

Kalani scowled down at Ahia. "Taking more than his share." With her left foot, she prodded three fat blocks of *pa'i 'ai* wrapped in coarse paper. "Taking what isn't his."

Liliha saw Ahia's dull, listless eyes. "He doesn't even know what he took."

Kalani bent down, her hand closing on the thin white hair

that straggled across the top of Ahia's head. She pulled his head up. Ahia's eyes bulged with sudden agony.

Without thinking, Liliha pulled the board over her shoulder and swung it forward. One of the long nails caught Kalani on the arm, piercing the dirty cotton of her sleeve, stabbing through skin and dragging a long, bloody furrow from her elbow to her wrist. Kalani howled and cradled her arm to her chest. Already the sleeve was bright with blood.

The strength went out of Liliha's hands and she dropped the board. If there were more splinters in her fingers and palms, she didn't feel them. "Ahia," she said, scrambling for him. Her hands seemed to move on their own. One hand snatched up the net; the other gripped Ahia's arm, pulling him after her. She and Ahia had to get away, *now,* while Kalani was clutching at her wound. They had to escape.

Escape? An awful voice chattered in Liliha's head. *Where?*

Ahia was on his feet now, stumbling, his eyes wet with tears of pain, one of his hands rubbing at his scalp. Liliha yanked at him until they were clear of the crowd. She stubbed her right big toe twice on rocks and muttered the pain beneath her breath, never breaking stride. Ahia looked like a filmy sheet of paper flapping behind her, his loose white shirt fluttering around his thin frame.

When Liliha glanced back, she couldn't see Kalani. The man was still packing supplies onto the handcart and, at the edge of the crowd, Opuhumanuu hunched, watching. Her rheumy eyes followed Liliha.

Liliha had seen the buildings of Kalaupapa settlement from a distance before, but she'd never stood among them. Now she pulled Ahia along the narrow path past the first house. A man sat in the doorway, smoking a pipe. He wore clean dungarees. Liliha stopped, turning to examine the half-dozen houses along the path. "Ahia," she panted. "Which one is it?"

Ahia stared at her. Sweat coated his face and darkened his shirt. Liliha still clutched one of his hands; it was burning hot. The man in the doorway plucked the pipe from his mouth and bent forward. His belly rested in his lap like an enormous stone. He jabbed the pipe stem at the third house down. "He lives in that one. Martha's house."

Liliha peered at it. "Is Hana there, do you know?" she asked.

"I saw her head over to Kalawao this morning. She goes to the hospital sometimes, to help out. She's a good woman." He grinned. "Better than the lot of us, I'd guess." The pipe stem jabbed at Ahia, who shrank back, his fingers plucking at his soiled mustache. "He's looking worse again, isn't he?"

Liliha tightened her grip on Ahia's slippery hand and tugged him along the path toward the house. Just as she reached the threshold, the door swung open and a woman leaned out, frowning. A hundred fine wrinkles etched the leaf-thin skin of her face. Her mouth was narrow, a cluster of black moles sprouting like tiny mushrooms near one corner.

"Ahia!" she snapped, and grabbed for his arm.

"He's sick," Liliha offered.

The woman's gaze scaled down Liliha, from her face to her dusty bare feet. Liliha crossed her arms over her chest, burrowing her fists deep in her armpits. Was the woman searching for signs of *ma'i pākē?* Her cool gaze returned to Liliha's face.

"Yes. He is sick."

"Is Hana here?"

"No."

Liliha spread one hand toward Ahia. "Is he all right?"

"He'll do." The woman nudged Ahia inside.

"Will he—?"

"I'll tend to him." The woman's moles quivered. The door shut.

Liliha backed away from the house.

"Are you from over at Kalawao?" asked the man with the pipe. She shook her head violently. She wasn't *from* Kalawao. She was from the island of Oahu. Kalawao wasn't her home and it never would be. The man looked puzzled, but said nothing.

She stared down the path toward the beach. She didn't see Kalani. "Are you one of the *kama'āina*?" she asked the man.

"Oh, yes." He grinned. "I've lived here all my life. My brother still lives here, too. We farm a little, raise some chickens and pigs."

"Don't you want to leave?"

"Leave Kalaupapa? This is my home."

Heart thudding, she nodded in the direction of Kalawao. "You aren't afraid of *them*?"

His eyes crinkled. "Afraid of the lepers? No. There are some that say their disease is a judgment from God, but I don't hold with that. I'm lucky, though. I've seen plenty of people with *ma'i pākē*, but my brother and I are still so healthy, I sometimes wonder if we're going to live forever."

As she left the Kalaupapa settlement, Liliha scanned the shore.

The sailors were rowing off. The crowds had broken apart. In the distance, the man pushed the handcart, laden with supplies. Liliha didn't see Kalani or Opuhumanuu. Clutching her net, she hurried toward the water though there probably wasn't any wood worth salvaging now. Was *her* board still on the sand where she'd dropped it? When Liliha imagined the nail slippery with blood, her stomach heaved into her throat. She felt even worse when she imagined the intensity of Kalani's hatred.

Motion to one side caught her eye, brought her to a dead stop. Manukekua was trudging along the shore. A narrow sack thrown across his shoulder jounced against his back at each step.

Liliha glanced at the beach once more. Maybe Kalani had left to clean out the cut and find something to bandage it with. Liliha sprang after Manukekua, waving one arm. He stopped to wait, but once she galloped up to him, she didn't know what to say. She stood there, panting and pulling her hair back from her face.

Manukekua bit at his lower lip.

"Is the Captain around?" Liliha asked.

He shook his head.

"Did you see where Kalani went?"

"No. But I was busy with other things." He let the sack he carried sag to the ground. Liliha pushed at the burlap with one foot. Something inside it slid. Glass struck glass with a faint clink. She glanced up questioningly. "You've seen him drink," Manukekua said. He bent forward and opened the sack, revealing jumbled bottles—amber, turquoise, green—filled with liquid. "Whiskey and rum. He hates kī beer. Won't drink it."

"Why?"

Manukekua shrugged. "Because Hawaiians brew it, I think." He tugged the sack closed. "Anyway, he likes whiskey best." This statement hung in the air.

"Where did you get them?" Liliha asked.

"One of the sailors. The Captain has an agreement with him. He brings more liquor every couple of months."

"They'll do that?"

"Sure. For a price."

Hope flared. Maybe she didn't need the minister or any of the people living at Kalaupapa to get a message out for her. She could give one of the sailors a message to give to her mother. She'd be willing to carve for weeks to make enough items to pay the sailor.

"What does the Captain give him?" she asked.

"Money."

"Always?"

"For as long as I've been the one picking up the bottles for him."

Liliha thought about that. "Do you think they'd take something else?"

"Like what?"

"Just . . . barter. Cups? Or bowls?"

He tilted his head to one side, watched her. "Like the things you've been making?"

Liliha looked up sharply. "You know about that?"

"I've seen you selling them. From the Captain's house."

"Oh." Liliha considered this. She was pleased and not sure

why she felt that way. "So do you think a sailor would take them?"

Manukekua shook his head.

"Why not?"

"The sailors are going back to Honolulu, back to the city. They want money. Anyway, what do you want them to get for you?"

"I want them to take something out."

Manukekua's eyebrows rose in surprise. "What?"

"Just . . ." Somehow, she felt like she could trust him. "A message."

"A message?"

"Yes."

"How?"

Her face burned. Voicing the idea made it seem too fragile, ridiculous. "I thought if I could give one of the sailors a message to take back home, he could get it there."

"Give it how?"

She spread her hands in confusion. "What?"

"Can you read or write?"

"I'd just say it to him."

Manukekua shook his head. "No. That won't work. Do you think they'll be able to remember more than a few words? And pass the message through *how* many people before it gets to your home? No."

She brooded over this. He was right, she saw that at once. But if she couldn't *tell* her message to a sailor, then how? A memory struck her then, Hana telling her that the woman named Martha sometimes sent letters to her sister. A letter. Of course. Then her message could be as long as she wanted and she wouldn't have to worry about anyone forgetting the words. She should have thought of it sooner.

She turned to Manukekua in excitement. "What if I sent a letter?"

"That could work," he said slowly.

"Can *you* read and write?"

He shook his head again.

"Who can?"

"Here? I don't know—the Captain."

Impossible. "Who else?"

"Nobody I know of."

"There has to be somebody."

"I don't know who."

She thought hard. Martha. Maybe Ahia, but he was so sick. Maybe Hana, but she'd be upset about what Liliha wanted to say in the letter. She might even refuse to finish the letter or to let her send it. But Martha—was she the woman with the moles who'd answered the door? If Liliha could work up the courage to ask her . . .

"I might have a way to get some money for you, if that would help," Manukekua said. "But I'm not sure when it would be. And I'd need some of your carvings."

Liliha looked at him with a mixture of curiosity and gratitude. "How?"

He waved the question aside. "But I don't know who could write the letter."

"I have an idea for *that*," Liliha answered, joy rising in her again.

Manukekua didn't ask whom she had in mind, just slung the sack over his shoulders. The bottles clanked.

"Manukekua." He stopped. Liliha took a deep breath. Her stomach felt strange again, not sick, but like it was full of air and light and was about to float away. Her face was hot. "I've looked for you. In the mornings when I've been at Kalawao."

His eyes brightened and his mouth curved in a tentative smile. "Really?"

Liliha nodded, smiling. Then she glanced down, embarrassed, and swung the net back and forth.

"Did you get rations this time?" Manukekua asked.

"*Pa'i 'ai* and salmon," she said. "Mine and Pauahi's."

"Is she good—?" He stopped. "Is she decent to you?"

"I have a roof over my head. A little food. Water to drink if I carry it. I earn every bit I get from her."

"She's honest, though."

"Hmm. But she'll push for every advantage."

"She's always been like that, but she's even worse now. It's hard to blame her. There are people here who have taken advantage of *her* because she's alone and it's so hard for her to walk."

"Like Kalani?"

His face tightened. "She's one."

Liliha lightly touched his hand. "I'm scared of her, too," she admitted.

"Most people are. And, I don't know why, Liliha, but she hates you."

Even though Liliha already knew this, hearing someone say it out loud brought fear buzzing into her head. "Anyway," she said, "Pauahi's all right."

Seconds passed before Manukekua's face eased. "You're sure?"

"She hates to have me selling things and her not getting anything out of it." She screwed up her face until it was as sour as Pauahi's and jabbed a finger hard against Manukekua's chest. "The girl uses *my* house to carve in. She sits on *my* dirt and she breathes *my* air. Why should she get all that for free? Hmm? *Hmm?*" Manukekua twisted away, laughing.

"She *does*," he gasped, bending forward, his hands braced flat against his thighs. He'd set his sack back on the ground. "She sounds just like that."

Liliha was laughing, too. Fear shrank into a small, hard ball deep in her belly, but it was still there. "The stingiest person I ever met. Except for my uncle."

"And Kalani," Manukekua added. "I used to work for her. *Slave* for her."

Liliha digested this. "When?"

"Right after I came here. I was alone, just like you."

"What about your parents?"

"They didn't come. My father was hardly around anyway. It was just my mother. She never noticed much of anything." He paused. "Not about me, anyway."

"Did somebody turn you in?"

"It was the woman who lived next to us. She spied on everybody and everything, and whatever she noticed, she told to the whole street. And to the policeman."

Liliha thought about this. "And nobody came with you?"

"No." His hands curled into fists. "There were two of us working for Kalani. *Working.* Fixing up the hut she'd taken from somebody else. Getting her water, keeping a garden, everything. And in return—well, we got a place to sleep on the floor sometimes if there was a really bad storm. Otherwise we slept outside, close by where we could hear her if she called, wanting something. We had enough food to live on. Barely. It was bad. The grown-ups would try to take all the rations. They'd just push kids out of the way." He looked up. "Stay away from Kalani, Liliha."

Liliha leaned closer. "Pauahi told me that Kalani killed a man."

"She's killed more than one."

Liliha's mouth went dry. She imagined that bloody furrow along Kalani's arm and Kalani's vengeance. *Why* did Ahia have to be there today? "Why did she kill the man?" she asked.

"Oh, he deserved it. She was pretty when she came here. Did you know that? It's hard to picture."

"Why did he deserve to be killed?"

"He attacked her." Manukekua's face reddened. "He made her be like his wife—but she *wasn't* his wife. And he beat her."

It's a strange place, isn't it? It's better to be ugly than beautiful. Liliha remembered Pauahi's words and tried to understand what Manukekua was telling her. She couldn't imagine Kalani letting someone beat her.

"He was a big man. Strong. So she waited until he got drunk on *kī* beer and passed out. Then she beat him to death."

"With a club?" Liliha thought of the club she'd seen Kalani wield that day.

"A board. I don't know where it came from. The fence, one of the crates for the food. They say he was nothing but bruises, purple and black from head to foot."

"Then what?"

"He got dumped in a grave. Nobody cared what happened to *his* body."

"And Kalani . . . ?"

"People were glad she'd gotten rid of that man. He'd bullied everybody. But then it was like Kalani couldn't stop. She kept on beating people and threatening them. You never could tell when she'd go into a rage."

"And Opuhumanuu? And that man I've seen with her?"

"The man helps her steal and lugs the food around and helps guard her hut. He gets his pick of the rations for his trouble. And who knows what else. He's got a mean streak, too, just like Kalani. But not as bad as her. Opuhumanuu might be all right if you got her away from Kalani. Anyway, I'd rather be around the Captain than any of them."

"He seems strange, too."

"He is, I guess. But he's not really so bad as long as I get my work done and stay out of his way when he's drunk." Liliha's dismay must have shown on her face, because Manukekua leaned toward her and touched her arm. "What else would you expect from a sea captain? My father said they are all roaring drunks. And he's a sailor, so he should know."

"Really? A sailor?"

Manukekua nodded eagerly. "That's what I was going to be,

too. Like my father. The way he used to talk about being out in the middle of the ocean and all the ports he'd been to. He'd show me the ships in Honolulu harbor. They were beautiful." Manukekua waved a hand inland. "So I always figured I'd work for a captain. Just not this way."

Liliha shook her head.

"So," Manukekua finished, "he's better than Kalani. Even Pauahi's better than Kalani."

"Pauahi doesn't matter anymore," Liliha said.

"She doesn't?"

"I'm not going to live with her much longer. I'm going to have my own hut."

"Your own . . . ?" Manukekua mulled this over, chewing his lip again. "Liliha, that's . . . are you sure you can—?"

She cut off the rest of his words. "I can't stay at Pauahi's forever. I don't *want* to. She's always watching me. Like she's trying to figure out how to get more work out of me." Liliha pointed *mauka*, inland toward the *pali*. The vegetation covering the cliff made it seem like a good place for keeping secrets or for hiding. "I want to build close to the *pali*. And east, so I won't have as far to go for water. If I build right in Wai'ale'ia Valley, I'd be by the stream. But I don't want to live there."

"No," Manukekua said, staring somberly at the *pali*. "No, too many bad things go on in the valley. People think they're hidden there. But the *pali*? You'll be more alone there. Wouldn't it be safer if you lived closer to the compound?"

"So the Captain can protect me?" Liliha scoffed. "Or the people dying in the hospital?"

"I would try to help you," Manukekua muttered, looking at his feet.

"And if the Captain's around? And awake? Then would you?" Manukekua's face darkened and Liliha wished she hadn't spoken.

"What about Kalani?" he said.

Liliha closed her eyes. She could see it: Kalani's ferocious skull looming above her in the darkness. "I don't think it's going to matter to Kalani where I live. Not if she hates me. She could come to the compound or to Pauahi's or to the foot of the *pali*."

Manukekua thought of another objection: "But if you leave Pauahi's, then you won't have her knife anymore. To carve with."

Could he see how stiff her smile was? "Oh, I have my own," she said. "My mother sent it here with me." Her stomach clenched. What if he wanted to see the knife? Had he noticed it missing from the Captain's house? "So, will you help me look for a good spot?" she hurriedly asked. "You know this place. That night during the storm it didn't seem to make any difference to you how dark it was, you knew where we were going."

"But the Captain—"

"Maybe when he's drunk?"

He nodded. "Yes. I can get away if he's drunk."

Liliha swung the net against her hip. "I go to the compound in the mornings sometimes. Or I'm at Pauahi's. So you know where to look for me."

"I'll find you."

Even her fear of Kalani couldn't destroy Liliha's excitement.

All the way back to Pauahi's, she kept breaking into a gallop. Is this what it was like to have a friend?

Pauahi looked up when she burst into the hut. "Is this all you got?" Pauahi asked, her mouth shriveling as she examined the rations. But Liliha only laughed at her and, plucking a rough wooden spoon from her sack, bounded outside again and across the field to a stone wall, where she sat down.

When she thought of the kindness in Manukekua's face, his gentle eyes, she found herself forgetting both the hunger and the fear that had accompanied her since she'd arrived on Molokai. She wanted to give Manukekua a present to thank him for helping her the night of the storm. To show him *she* was *his* friend.

She held the spoon's half-formed handle close to her face. This spoon would be her gift. Maybe, somehow, using the knife to make a present for Manukekua would mean her theft wasn't such a bad thing. She closed her eyes to imagine how she'd carve the handle into a ship like the ones she'd seen in the harbor the day she went into exile. When she opened her eyes again, the air seemed to glitter with miniature wooden ships that tossed playfully, heading out to sea, and home.

CHAPTER NINE

TWO WEEKS PASSED BEFORE, ONE MORNING, LILIHA STRODE into the compound with her sack of carvings and saw Manukekua leaning against the *pū hala* tree. He ducked his head in a quick welcome.

"Whiskey?" she asked.

"He's dead asleep from it."

"You think he'll sleep for a long time?" she asked.

Manukekua nodded. "He woke up early, right before dawn, but when I tried to give him something to eat, he just roared for more whiskey. So . . . if you still want help looking for a place to build your hut . . ."

Liliha grinned. Excitement blazed through her at the thought of finally beginning construction. The sooner they started, the sooner they'd finish and she could not only leave Pauahi, but have a snug shelter ready when her mother came. Still, she figured the time hadn't been wasted. She'd been carving every minute she could, trusting that Manukekua really would know a way to get money for the objects she made.

"I was starting to think you'd be trapped inside with the Captain forever," she said. "I was going to go hunt out a spot tomorrow by myself if I didn't see you today."

"Good thing he got into the whiskey, then."

"There's another place I wanted to show you. It's out away from the *pali*." Her fingers breezed across Manukekua's arm.

"Are you *sure* you don't want to live closer to the compound?" Manukekua cautioned. "Because I really think—"

"I told you, no. I don't need anyone else there with me. It's not like I could count on anybody to help me."

Manukekua made protesting noises, but Liliha ignored them and rummaged through her sack. She kept her head lowered. "I have something for you," she said. Her stomach seemed to slip sideways. What if he thought her gift was ugly? What if he laughed?

"Open your hands," she instructed, drawing the spoon free and placing it on Manukekua's flat palms. He held it gingerly, as if he was afraid he might splinter the wooden sails or snap the tiny masts. He brought it close to his face.

Liliha explained, "A doctor at Kalihi Hospital told me stories about pirates and ghost ships. He told me how ships looked, all the sails full. And then I saw the boats in the harbor. I thought it would remind you of home and . . ." Her voice trailed off. Why did he have to examine the carving with such intensity? His nose practically touched the handle.

"You made a crow's nest!"

"The doctor told me a story about a skeleton that stood watch for a hundred years in the crow's nest of a ship. But the ship was just a ghost, too; the real ship sank in a storm."

Manukekua tucked the spoon into his pants pocket. "I'll use it tonight." He ducked his head, a pleased smile warming his face. "Thank you."

Liliha smiled back at him. Relief flooded her, and gratitude that he seemed so happy with the present, with something she'd created.

The ground rose gradually under their feet. Liliha pulled ahead. She glanced back once to see Manukekua looking around, his shoulders hunched forward, alert. A great round crater opened at the center of the peninsula. A ridge of earth circled the crater, as if holding danger away. Liliha clambered to the top of the ridge.

"Have you been here?" Liliha asked, looking back at Manukekua. "I found it a couple of days ago when I was looking for wood. It might not be a bad spot to build. I know I was talking about the *pali*, but you can see all the way to the ocean from here. I'd be able to see whenever boats came, even before I'd hear the whistle. You can see a long way in every direction."

"And people can see you from every direction, too," Manukekua pointed out.

"I—yes. I guess they can."

Manukekua pointed to a hut midway to the shore. "Do you know who lives there?" Liliha shook her head. "Kalani."

Without thinking, Liliha bent slightly forward, ducked her head. She stared at the hut. It was larger than Pauahi's and, from a distance, looked equally sturdy. At any rate, it stood upright and it still had a roof and walls thick with thatch, which made it superior to most of the huts on the peninsula. A man squatted just outside the doorway. Liliha thought it was the man she'd seen before with Kalani.

Was he looking back at Liliha and Manukekua? Liliha froze,

wondering if Kalani was inside the hut and if the man would alert her. But he didn't move, just continued his watch.

Liliha half-slid down the crater's interior wall; it was steep at first, but gradually leveled out. Manukekua skidded after her.

"That's one of his jobs," Manukekua said, his voice dropping to a whisper even though the man was much too distant to hear. "Guarding Kalani's hut."

Liliha's gaze darted up to the ridge. "Where do you think she is?"

Manukekua pressed a hand against Liliha's back; his touch was comforting.

"I saw her earlier. She was heading toward Wai'ale'ia. Not carrying any buckets, though."

"No," Liliha said slowly, her fear easing slightly. "She wouldn't carry her own water, would she? Maybe this isn't such a good place to build." She kneeled beside the water that filled the bottom of the crater. "Anyway, the water's not fresh, is it? Otherwise people would bring their buckets here. Did you know there was a lake here?" She dipped her fingers into the water.

"Don't do that." Manukekua gripped her wrist, his thin fingers iron hard. Startled, Liliha turned toward him. He held her hand against his chest. "This is a bad place."

"A bad place?"

He slowly let go of her hand. "There are bodies in that water."

"Bodies?" She sprang up. "Lepers?"

"Some. But I've heard that the people who lived here before us used to sink their dead into this water."

Liliha pressed her hands together.

"I've seen it, Liliha. Bodies sunk here. When people don't want to bother digging a grave." He turned away and started up the slope, soon disappearing past the ridge. Liliha scrambled after him. He was already walking away from the crater and in the direction opposite Kalani's hut. The sun caught at his face, making the sore on his cheek glisten like the wet shining silver of a snail's path. It was longer and deeper now.

"It's so exposed here anyway," he said, turning back to her. "The wind would be bad *all* the time." He managed a smile. "Not just most of the time. And it's no hiding place."

"I want a home, not a hiding place." Liliha's voice thickened. Tilting her head back, she said, "Closer to the *pali,* then."

They turned to the towering green cliff. If she lived at their feet, would she feel like she was trapped in the shadow of a prison? Or would she feel sheltered?

"You'd still be alone," Manukekua pointed out.

"I will be anyway."

"Is there anyone who could live with you?"

It still hurt to think about Hana's refusal to let her live at the Kalaupapa settlement. It hardly mattered that Liliha understood Hana's reasons. The hurt remained.

Liliha shook her head.

"Are you sure?"

"There was one woman, but she and her husband found somewhere good to live."

"Good?" Manukekua asked skeptically.

"Well . . . not bad."

Manukekua smiled at that though Liliha could tell he was still concerned about her living alone.

Liliha hadn't seen Hana come to the hospital for days now. What if Hana was sick, too? More likely, it was Ahia. Even though Liliha was disappointed that Hana wanted her to live the rest of her life in the leper colony, she still didn't want to think of either Hana or Ahia suffering. She vowed to go to Kalaupapa landing soon to find out what had happened.

They cut across a field and caught a trail that meandered through weeds. The trail narrowed as they approached the *pali*.

"What about over here?" Liliha said, pushing off through a thick growth of *kī* and dark green *naio* shrubs. "There's already a sort of clearing." The airy leaves of the *kiawes* were high enough that they wouldn't interfere with a roof, but would provide shade and some protection from wind and rain. Liliha turned in a slow circle: On one side stood the *pali* and the narrow trail winding toward it; in all other directions she saw brush, sky, flat plain, a few trees. If her mother came down the *pali*, she wouldn't have to walk far from the bottom of the cliff to get to Liliha's hut.

She closed her eyes and imagined falling asleep here at night. It would be cool, maybe too cool, but the wind would make a gentle, shushing sound in the leaves.

She opened her eyes. "This is where I'll build."

Manukekua's eyes cut toward the *pali*. "I still don't think—"

Liliha stepped back onto the trail and followed it until it began to ascend. Excitement flushed her face. "I can see the ocean from up here," she called back. "You see? I'll have the *pali* and the ocean." She saw that Manukekua wanted to raise more objections. His mouth opened, but he stopped when he saw the joy on Liliha's face.

"Liliha, are you sure?"

She could only nod.

"Then all we need to do," Manukekua said, relenting, "is build it."

CHAPTER TEN

LILIHA WAS SO EAGER TO START ON THE HUT THAT, AFTER fetching water the next morning, she hurried to the spot she'd chosen and began to clear the earth. She drew the knife out from a deep pocket she'd sewn on the front of her skirt. Use of the needle and thread necessary for the job had cost her a day's rations and considerable griping from Pauahi.

Before she could build, she had to slice away any weeds and vines that twisted across the dirt where her floor would be. The plants were stubborn, the vines rubbery and resistant. It took her an hour to finish the section, roughly six square feet, in front of her. She then shifted a few feet away and began to hack at another tangle of weeds.

The morning was humid, moisture shimmering the air. Liliha pushed up her sleeves. By noon, her shirt was soaked, the fabric pasted to her skin. She concentrated so hard that she didn't notice Manukekua until he crouched down beside her.

"It's a good day to start," he said, examining the cloudless sky.

"I'm glad you could get away!" Liliha told him, smiling. Pushing out her lower lip, she blew a thin stream of breath upward, riffling the damp hairs that clung to her forehead. "It's good that it's sunny. I couldn't stand to wait. It was bad enough taking time this morning to go get water." She shoved a mass of fibrous vine to one side and turned toward Manukekua. He was staring at Liliha's hand, his mouth open with surprise. She looked down.

The knife. Her fingers clenched around the handle. Sticky sap oozed along the blade. Manukekua's gaze flickered from the knife to her face. Their eyes caught.

"It's my . . ." She stopped. *It's my knife,* she'd meant to say. *The knife my mother sent with me.* But the words wouldn't pass through her dry throat.

Before she could speak, Manukekua looked away and slowly said, "Maybe we can get all this cleared away today. That would be a good start." He reached into a clump of grass, rummaged at the base of it, yanked the grass up by the roots.

"Manukekua." Liliha's face was hot. *Are you his friend or aren't you?* The question clamored in her head. "It's your knife," she blurted, hardly able to believe the secret words were out in the open. "I took it. That first night. I'm sorry. I didn't want to get you in trouble."

He stared at the weeds a moment, his hands still. Then he reached forward and tugged at another clump. "It's all right."

"Did the Captain—was he angry?"

Manukekua's mouth quirked up at one corner. "I don't think he even noticed. But I wondered what happened to it." He tossed a jumble of weeds over his shoulder.

Liliha extended the knife toward him. "You can have it back."

He turned to face her. He was smiling. Liliha trembled with sudden relief. Manukekua really *wasn't* angry with her.

"You keep it," he said.

She wanted to grip the knife hard and pull it safely out of his reach. What would she do without the knife? But she forced her hand to be still. "If the Captain *does* notice, if he gets mad at you . . ." She quailed at the thought of the Captain, red-faced and furious, his voice booming, his eyes lunatic. "He could do something terrible to you."

"He could. But if he hasn't noticed the knife by now—"

"He could hurt you, Manukekua!"

"He's not so bad."

"I don't believe that!"

Manukekua raised his hands, palms up. Long white scars crisscrossed the skin.

"The Captain?" Liliha whispered, horrified. She traced the hardened ridge of one scar with a fingertip.

"No. Kalani. See? The Captain's nothing next to her. The Captain gets mad, he gets drunk and confused, but he isn't cruel. Kalani likes to hurt people."

"When did she do this?" Liliha asked.

"Remember, I told you I was her servant when I first came here, me and another boy? One night there was a storm and I tried to sneak inside, even though she'd told me and the other boy to stay out. I didn't *want* to go inside, but it was so miserable in the mud, all that rain. And the other boy—he was scared of lightning. He thought we could sneak inside for a couple of hours, just inside the door, till the lightning stopped and we'd dried off. Then we'd sneak back out again."

"But Kalani was awake?"

"Not until he stumbled into a pot and knocked it over. She was furious. She held my hands down on the table and slashed them. Like that." He made a slicing motion along each of the scars.

Liliha shivered. "And the other boy?"

He paused. "She hit him. I saw that. Then she dragged him outside. I waited and waited, it seemed like hours, crouching at the door, my hands bleeding all over my pants. Kalani was alone when she came back."

"So where was the other—?"

Manukekua cut her off. "I didn't see him again. But she said she killed him. She said she clubbed him on the head and knocked him out and then she threw him in the lake. In the crater."

Liliha could hardly breathe. "Do you really think she did that?"

"I never saw him again."

"Not ever?"

He shook his head.

"Did everybody else think she killed him?"

"Yes."

"And you stayed with her?" Liliha could hardly imagine staying with someone who'd slashed her hands open. But then Grandmother had had her own style of viciousness. And Liliha had put up with that.

"I stayed till the Captain came. The other kids here were all Hawaiian. My father was a *haole,* an American sailor. The Captain doesn't like Hawaiians, so when he wanted someone to wait on him, he chose me." Manukekua paused. When he spoke again, his voice was thoughtful. "Most of the time he just ignores me, as long as I get the work done. He gives me enough food, too. I wouldn't want to cross him, but he treats me all right."

"What's *wrong* with the Captain?"

Manukekua hesitated, rubbing at his lower lip. "The Captain . . . when he's drunk, he talks a lot sometimes. Sometimes it's just rambling, I don't know what he's saying. But other times he says things about when he was growing up or about being in the Navy and fighting. Something about a ship burning and it was his fault. His ship. Once he said something about a wife and he was crying, begging for her to forgive him for leaving. Sometimes it seems like he thinks he's still in charge of a ship. Still fighting a war."

Liliha shut her eyes, but instead of envisioning the Captain, she saw Manukekua, younger and even thinner, bent over a table while Kalani lowered a knife to his hand, the blade flashing silver and blue every time lightning blasted outside the doorway.

"So . . ." Manukekua grasped Liliha's hand, tightening her fingers around the knife handle. His own fingers were warm and damp. "You keep it."

Her face burned. She lowered her head in thanks. Manukekua released her hand, and she immediately began tearing the blade through the vegetation. From the corner of her eye, she saw Manukekua reach for another fistful of weeds.

They labored until late afternoon, speaking little but working easily side by side. When the clearing was completely bare, they stamped the earth smooth and hard.

Liliha sank back and looked with satisfaction at the cleared earth. "Tomorrow, I'll start on a frame." She wiped the back of her hand across her mouth, smearing dirt on her chin and her cheeks, and squinted at the sky. Scarlet and violet streaked the clouds.

"It's getting late," Manukekua said. "I should go back, too."

He walked with her a short ways before they separated, Manukekua heading for the compound and Liliha to Pauahi's.

A fire struggled to keep itself alive in front of Pauahi's hut. Liliha glanced down at it, irritated. That was so typical of Pauahi, to cook her own meal and then leave the fire to die before Liliha could use it.

Liliha ducked to pass through the doorway. The hut's interior was gloomy, shadows swelling from the corners. A single dim strip of twilight angled in from the doorway and cut across the floor. Pauahi sat with her back pressed against the wall, her face a dark stone. Her eyes snapped open, following Liliha's progress into the room.

Liliha crouched in the corner where she slept each night. She opened the neck of her sack, then paused to look across at Pauahi. Something shone dimly on Pauahi's cheeks. Liliha stared, trying to figure out what it was. Impossible to imagine that Pauahi had been crying. Liliha took a step forward.

Blood. A thin line of blood oozed from a long, vertical cut in the middle of each of Pauahi's cheeks.

"You can't stay here anymore," Pauahi said dully.

"What happened?" Liliha crouched beside her and reached to touch one of the wounds. Pauahi's arms flew up to push Liliha away. Liliha stood and looked around the room, trying to figure out what had happened. Pauahi's supplies were nearly gone—almost all her leaves, vines, bowls. One of the water buckets was turned on its side, a tongue of water stretching from the rim across the dirt.

"What happened?"

"You have to leave here now."

"But . . . ?" Liliha spread her hands out helplessly. "Who will carry water for you? Or get your rations?"

"I'll find someone. I always have. Do you think you can't be replaced?"

"But what—?" Before Liliha could finish, Pauahi heaved herself to her feet and shuffled outside. Liliha could hear her muttering and poking at the fire. Liliha thought of her new hut, nothing more than a packed dirt floor at this point. She leaned out of the doorway.

"Pauahi?"

The woman just shook her head in Liliha's direction, then ignored her.

"Pauahi!" Hopeless. Pauahi wouldn't talk to her. Liliha ducked inside again and kneeled by her sack, packing her few possessions. As she slid each item into the sack, she muttered: "Cup. Ribbon. Skirt."

She set the sack down and glanced around. Where was the bowl she'd carved just a couple of days earlier? And the spoon she'd finished last week, the one with the handle shaped like a dolphin? She shoved aside Pauahi's sleeping mats, rooted through the few remaining vines and blocks of *pa'i 'ai,* the single cooking pot. Nothing.

Liliha spun around and darted outside.

"Where are they?" she demanded. "Who cut your face?" When Pauahi didn't answer, Liliha bent down, gripped the front of Pauahi's shirt, and shook her. *"Where are they?"*

"Wait!" Pauahi cried. "Wait. I didn't take them. It was Kalani. She has them."

Liliha released Pauahi's shirt and rocked back. Her arms trembled and her breath shook. She rubbed the back of one hand across her damp forehead. "Kalani? What is Kalani doing with them?"

Pauahi glanced around as if half-expecting Kalani to appear. "She came here today to ask for presents. 'Tokens,' she calls them. Tokens!" She looked up at Liliha and shrugged in half-hearted apology. "She said she wanted the bowl and the spoon. What else was I supposed to do? She laughed at the dolphin."

"When did she cut your face?"

Pauahi raised her hands to her cheeks; they came away with blood on the fingertips. "She said I had it coming to me for letting a thief like you stay here." Pauahi looked at the blood for a moment before wiping her fingers on her skirt. "She never took so much before." Pauahi's face squeezed tight. The loss of calabashes and leaves for weaving mats seemed to upset her more than her own wounds. "She was never so angry before. It's because of you."

"Me?"

"I don't know what you did to her, but she hates you. It's a terrible hatred. If I'd known that—"

"You never would have let me set foot in your house."

"You can't stay here. I've tried to do what I could for you. But you're a danger. You have to leave."

"Pauahi—"

"I told you, you can't stay here." Pauahi turned her back.

Liliha finally ducked inside again and drew her sack shut. She stood, surveying the room. It was ridiculous. She'd wanted to get away from Pauahi, but now that she was being forced out, she was scared to go.

"I suppose you could take a *little* of the beef there." Pauahi's voice startled Liliha and she swung around to see the woman stooped in the doorway. Pauahi raised a crooked finger. "Back there in the corner. But not more than a quarter of it, mind you. And nothing else. Ever." She disappeared outside.

Liliha squatted in the corner behind Pauahi's sleeping mats, unwrapped the narrow block of dried beef, sliced off a quarter section with her knife, and dropped the beef into her sack.

"Thank you," she told Pauahi, pausing beside the dead fire. Pauahi stared resolutely toward the sea and the darkening sky and didn't answer.

Liliha slung the sack lightly over her shoulder and hurried toward the *pali* and the shadows gathering beneath it.

CHAPTER ELEVEN

LILIHA HOPED TO SLEEP SOUNDLY THAT NIGHT, ESPECIALLY after eating Pauahi's dried beef. For once, a meal almost filled her belly.

She curled up on the cleared patch of dirt, her sack clutched against her chest. The ground was cool, the wind strong. Liliha rolled from side to side. She couldn't stop thinking about Pauahi's slashed cheeks and Manukekua's hands, or imagining Kalani creeping through the brush at the foot of the *pali,* a club brandished in one hand, ready to smash Liliha's skull to pieces.

Her right foot bothered her as well, the sole prickling strangely and the bones aching. She didn't sleep until dawn. When she woke, her muscles were stiff and her head heavy. She pulled a small chunk of salted salmon from her sack, ate it, then set to work making a frame for the house.

She worked alone for the next three days, stopping occasionally to eat from her small store of rations and fish. Twice she walked to Wai'ale'ia, drank deeply from the stream, filled two cups she'd already carved from driftwood, and carried them back with her.

She hacked long, supple branches from a young *koa* tree. Then she sank down and worked the tip of the knife into the earth, widening the hole and deepening it several inches until the thick end of one *koa* branch just fit inside it. She packed soil hard around the branch so that it stood firm and upright. She repeated this until she'd made a circle of branches springing from similar holes. The circle was about ten feet in diameter.

On the fourth day, she cut down *kī* growing near the *pali's* base, braided cords from the stems and leaves, and tied the cords around the circle of poles. She'd finished the frame of the hut.

Manukekua didn't appear again until the following afternoon. Liliha sat within the framework, pulling long stems of *pili* grass from the mound beside her and bundling them into the thick rectangles that would hang from the horizontal lashings and so shingle the hut.

Manukekua dropped down next to her. "Sorry," he said. "I couldn't get here before. The Captain . . ." He tilted his head back. "You did all this already? It looks good." He poked a finger at one of the *koa* branches. "Strong."

Liliha nodded. She was proud of the work she'd done so far. The framework was trim and sturdy.

Manukekua grabbed a handful of loose grass and tried to knot the ends together.

"Like this." Liliha raised her hands in front of him and slowed her fingers.

Manukekua glanced at her. "We didn't build houses this way in Honolulu." He smiled. "Not that I ever built any kind of house." He glanced again at the small stack of finished shingles and then at the frame. "It's going to take a while to finish, isn't it?"

"I want to make sure these are thick enough to keep the wind and rain out."

He nodded. "That's a good idea." He tried to copy the movements Liliha's fingers made. He worked slowly, his head bent low over his hands, his mouth tight with concentration.

Liliha worked mechanically, trying to decide whether or not to tell him about Kalani's attack on Pauahi. He was her friend; he deserved the truth. But the truth would make him worry. He'd probably want her to abandon the hut and try to find other people to live with: at the hospital maybe, or crowded in some rotten hut with half a dozen sufferers who would expect her to fetch and cook and clean for them. *No.*

"Manukekua? I wanted to ask you for a favor."

"What?"

"Pauahi won't let me stay with her anymore."

His head shot up; the tangled grass dropped, forgotten, to his lap. "Won't let—?"

Liliha held up a hand. "It's all right. Really. I'm sleeping here instead. I just want to get the hut finished before any more bad storms hit."

"Why won't she let you stay there?"

"I'm not sure." She forced herself to meet his eyes. "Maybe she decided I was too lazy." She turned her attention to Manukekua's misshapen grass bundle. "Like *this.*" She put her hands on top of his, guiding their movements. "You see?"

He nodded, his fingers continuing to work the grass awkwardly. But his eyes held suspicion. "I can't imagine she thinks you're lazy, Liliha."

"Well, who knows what was in her head?" Liliha said with a small, unconcerned shrug, and tried to change the subject. "But, anyway, Manukekua, I have a favor to ask of you. I need a bucket to carry water. I don't have a big enough piece of wood to make one."

Manukekua's eyes grew thoughtful. "Would Pauahi trade one of hers?"

"No. She only has two. She wouldn't give up one of them."

"Maybe for the knife?"

Liliha's face burned at the mention of the knife. "I'm not trading that."

Manukekua gnawed his lower lip. "I can't give you any of the Captain's. I *can't*, Liliha."

"Who else would have an extra?" She knew, even as she asked, how ridiculous the question was. The only "extras" that the lepers of Kalaupapa possessed were extra hunger, extra disease, extra misery. "Well, who'd have more than one?"

"Kalani," Manukekua promptly answered, raising his hands at Liliha's dismay. "Or anyone who doesn't mind stealing from other people."

Liliha's cheeks grew hot again. She wondered if Manukekua was thinking about the knife. He stared hard at the ground, but as if he didn't really see it.

"I can't ask Kalani to trade with me," Liliha protested.

"No. But we could try to take a bucket from her."

"Take it?" Liliha was startled. She hadn't expected Manukekua to suggest theft.

"The way she took it from someone else."

Liliha pondered this. All right, maybe Kalani deserved it. But if she found out who had dared to steal from her, her revenge would be terrible. "What about the man?"

"He can't be there every second. Neither can Opuhumanuu. Not when there are sick people to bully and steal from."

"But you can't be sure," Liliha pointed out. "Any one of them might be there. Or all of them."

"If I keep a lookout over the wall of the crater—"

"No," she insisted.

"I'll get one for you, I promise," Manukekua said. "Can you wait till tomorrow? I'll bring it to you here."

"But *where* will you get it?" Liliha demanded. She imagined Kalani attacking him, his face cut open, his palms hacked and bloody. Her stomach shrank with dread.

Manukekua's smile was slow and not entirely steady. "Don't worry. I'll get one."

She was certain then that he would try to take one from Kalani. "No. Don't do it."

"It'll be all right," he said.

"No, you don't understand." Her hands were agitated, fluttering at the air. "If she catches you—"

"I won't let her."

Liliha grabbed Manukekua's hands, forced them open, and rubbed her fingers across the scars. "Pauahi made me leave because of Kalani. When Kalani found out I was living there, she cut Pauahi's cheeks open." Liliha dropped Manukekua's hands and ran her fingertips down his face. "Like this. She'd do the same thing to you. Or worse."

He gripped her wrists, stared hard at her face. "I knew it."

"Knew what?"

"You shouldn't be living here alone, Liliha."

Pulling free, she stepped back, shook her head with impatience. "I'm not going to live in the hospital. Or beg somebody to let me be her servant."

"But if you'd—"

"We've already talked about this."

Guilt shadowed his face. "I'd let you stay at the Captain's if I could."

Liliha waved that suggestion away, trying not to show her fear. "If she wants to come after me, she will."

"Liliha—"

"But there's no point trying to steal something right from her hut. She'd *kill* us for that, either one of us."

Manukekua finally nodded simple acknowledgment.

Liliha glanced at the sky. "Anyway," she said, "I'll still go to Wai'ale'ia today. Whether I have a bucket or not. I *have* to get something to drink. And I can wash all *this* off." She spread out her hands, which were caked with dirt and dried sweat, the fingernails black.

"I can try to get you a cup of water at the Captain's," Manukekua said in a rush. "If he's still asleep."

"I'll find a bucket," Liliha said.

"Where?"

"I have an idea." She wouldn't tell him more than that except to promise that she wouldn't try to steal anything from Kalani.

They worked hard until late afternoon, weaving and knotting the grass into sturdy bundles, which they hung upon the cords lashed about the hut's frame. Manukekua was quiet and kept glancing at Liliha from the corner of his eyes. He looked embarrassed, but she didn't know if he was ashamed of not being able to find a bucket easily or of his failure to offer one of the Captain's.

When he left, he moved away swiftly, his bare feet crushing the stems and flattening the leaves of *kī* plants alongside the trail. Liliha waited until she couldn't see him anymore before she set out alone in search of a bucket.

CHAPTER TWELVE

THE HOSPITAL.

Liliha remembered the bucket containing stagnant water and the ladle fallen beside it, the dying man struggling to get a drink.

If there was only the one bucket, *of course* she wouldn't take it. Of course not. But if they had one, they might have more, and she could borrow one, just for a little while, just until she was able to find a large block of wood (*where?* A voice in her head challenged her) and make her own. She remembered how sick the people on the hospital floor had been: beyond food or water, most of them. Beyond any help or comfort. They wouldn't miss a bucket.

And she'd return it in just a few days. She would.

She paused in front of the building. Her gaze flitted between the shut door and the closed windows. Hana must not be there, because if she were, she would have tried to air the room. Liliha was ashamed of her relief. Guilt pricked at her. She had worked so hard on the house that she still hadn't gone to see Hana. The truth was, she was afraid to see Ahia again. Afraid to see him sick the way he'd been that day on the beach. And she was afraid of the anger she would feel if Hana started talking again about how Kalaupapa was Liliha's real home.

Reaching for the doorknob, she hoped that no other *kōkuas* were inside tending to their dying relatives. At least there was no doctor to worry about.

She stumbled two blind steps into the room, stood blinking. The few forlorn medicine bottles still stood on the shelves. A spray of shriveled wildflowers drooped from the neck of an empty liquor bottle. The dead flowers did nothing to lessen the stench.

Liliha clamped the back of one hand against her mouth and nose, fighting nausea. She squinted down the length of the murky room. Each patient had a grass mat now; someone— probably Hana—had seen to that. But some of the mats were filthy and some patients sprawled off of them and onto the floor. Not everyone had a blanket. The room was warm and damp, but several patients clutched blankets to their chins and shivered, while others, coated with sweat, peevishly plucked their shirts open. Liliha tried to avert her gaze from the ruined flesh, the sunken noses, and filmy eyes.

Still, she couldn't help seeing the patients at the edge of her vision. With a shock, she realized she'd seen one of them before: the man covered with sores who had mocked and cursed Ahia that first day in the compound. He sprawled on the floor, his eyes rolled white up into his head. Liliha hugged herself. It was terrifying to think of how his condition had worsened in just two months. He'd looked ill that first day, but *now* . . . His cracked lips muttered something incomprehensible. Liliha shut her ears to the sound and to the noise of someone in shadows at the far end of the room who was crying.

Where were the buckets? Liliha glanced around wildly, trying to remember where she'd seen one before. Had it been near the door or not? She inched forward, curling her toes under as if that gave her some sort of perch, separating her from the misery and stink.

Then she saw it: a rust-eaten bucket shoved against a wall between two mats. Was it the same bucket she'd seen before? She crept closer to it, trying to escape the notice of the woman and the young boy curled on mats beside it. Neither of them moved. Liliha stooped over the bucket, ran a fingertip along the furry rim, being careful not to cut herself on the jagged edges. The very thought of having something to drink made her realize how parched she was.

She peered at the water. Dirt and drowned gnats flecked the surface. No ladle. She pushed the fingers of one hand into the water and stirred them around, raised her dripping fingers to her mouth and pressed them to her tongue. The slight moisture sharpened her thirst.

There had to be a second bucket. There *had* to be. Then it would be all right to take this one. But she needed to find it quickly; the deeper she moved into the room, the more the stench overwhelmed her.

Liliha rushed through the room until she found she'd returned to the single, rusty pail. She stooped. The handle squeaked as she pulled it upright and lifted the bucket. Her hands shook.

They won't use it anyway. They're dying, all of them—and soon.

There was a patient watching her. He sat on a mat at the far end of the room. He was skinny and young and he'd dragged himself partially upright against the wall, his head tilted back, his bare legs sticking out from beneath a worn blanket. He stared at Liliha, his dark eyes glittering with fever. His mouth hung open and he took quick, shallow breaths.

Panic surged through Liliha. She crooked her arms around the bucket and held it to her chest. Had he seen her take it? Did he know it wasn't hers? Those glittering eyes didn't break away, and Liliha finally edged toward the man. No one else even glanced at her.

When he reached up for her with one hand, Liliha fell back a step. Her stomach folded over on itself. "Did you . . . ?" She took a breath. "Did you need something?" Surely he didn't think she was a *kōkua*. She couldn't help him. That was what Hana did—Hana, who wasn't here today and who obviously hadn't been here in days.

The man struggled to speak, sweat oozing from his face.

"Maybe Hana will be in tomorrow," Liliha said. "She can help you."

"Hana?" the man rasped. He shook his head delicately as if even that slight motion hurt. "They brought me here last night. In the dark. Someone. Someone—I don't know who . . ." His gaze swung blankly around the room. "Can you help me? My leg hurts." Before Liliha could speak, the man reached for her again and groaned, "It's my leg. Please, it hurts."

"I'm not . . . Hana's the—" Liliha protested, then stopped, her mouth opening in astonishment. The man's legs seemed to be moving. Not the legs themselves, but the skin. At first she couldn't identify what she was seeing, and she bent closer.

Liliha leaped back so violently that she lost her footing and staggered against the wall. Water splashed over the rim of the bucket still tight in her arms, soaking the front of her shirt. The man had stopped looking at her. Fever consumed him and his eyes rolled white in their sockets. "Nurse," he whined. "Nurse, my *legs . . .*"

Liliha broke down the aisle at a run, water sloshing onto the floor. She threw the door shut behind her and fell, panting, against it. The bucket thumped to the ground, spiraling onto its side and spilling the last of the water. No wonder his legs hurt. And no wonder she'd imagined the skin was moving. It wasn't the *skin* moving, but maggots, almost luminous in the gloom, squirming and writhing in the open wounds that covered his legs.

Liliha gulped at the air until her nausea eased. It seemed to her that the hospital's reek still tinged the air around her. Finally, she bent down to pick up the bucket and scuttled from the compound. She knew she must look guilty.

The light was already fading as she walked to Wai'ale'ia. At the stream, she gulped handfuls of water and splashed her face clean. She rinsed the bucket and filled it. Then she bent to scrub her feet. But when she reached to wash the sole of her right foot, she stopped in confusion, then rubbed harder. She could feel only the faintest pressure from her hand against the ball of her foot. She pulled her foot out of the water and tried to twist it around to see the bottom. The skin was wrinkled from the water, but she couldn't tell if it had the same discolored patches that her arms had. She swished it cautiously about.

For a moment, it seemed that the whole world spiraled into a funnel, the spout pointing directly at her foot. A sick dread filled her stomach. Her fingers fidgeted on the handle of her knife. What would happen if she sliced a thin layer of skin from her foot? Would the skin beneath be sensitive to heat and cold and wet? She shook her head. She'd seen a man at Kalihi Hospital in Honolulu who'd sliced out coins of numb flesh from his arms and legs as if he could pare away the disease and avoid exile. It hadn't worked.

She was panic-stricken. Is this how it had begun for the man at the hospital with the maggots roiling in his legs? An itch, an ache, a numb patch on the sole of one foot? Shoving herself back from the stream, she ground her right foot into the dirt, hoping to feel the soil's warmth. She felt nothing.

How long before sores covered her legs? How long before maggots came? Liliha froze in place. She whimpered. What had that man at Kalaupapa landing said to her after she'd helped Ahia home? That some people looked at leprosy as a judgment from God on those who sinned. She gazed down at the bucket through a blur of tears. She'd stolen it. Not borrowed it. And left those too sick to walk with nothing at all to drink. Her nose ran and she swiped her sleeve across it.

Still crying, Liliha gripped the bucket, now heavy with water. She would have to walk cautiously from now on. If she accidentally cut her foot within that numb patch, she'd never feel it. She thought about the shoes she'd seen people at Kalihi Hospital wear, the doctors and nurses and government officials. The missionaries had worn shoes, too. Liliha never had, but now she wished she owned a pair. She'd never noticed before just how rough the ground was, how many fragments of rock and sharp sticks lay scattered across it. Suddenly it struck her as astonishing that *anyone* could walk barefoot and not end up with gashes sunk deep into their feet.

She inched her way to the trail, her eyes fixed on the ground, scanning for thorns and pebbles. How long would it take to walk to her house this way? Each time she stepped forward with her right foot, she caught her breath, praying to Hana's god, the missionaries' god, to *any* god that she would feel *something*. Even pain. But the skin might as well have been dead already.

Where could she get shoes? Who even wore them, besides the Captain with his thick leather boots? The Captain, yes, and Ahia. She tried to picture Ahia as he'd looked the morning they'd arrived at Kalaupapa: white shirt, dark trousers, a pair of smudged, black shoes. If Ahia had an extra pair of shoes— they'd be too big for Liliha, of course, but she could stuff rags or weeds in the toes and heels—or maybe Hana had brought a pair that she didn't bother to wear.

That night, she drank only a single mouthful of water from the bucket; somehow, it seemed to her that if she forced herself to remain thirsty, made her throat ache with it, if she suffered along with the wretches at the hospital, then taking the bucket wouldn't be quite so terrible. She kept prodding at the numb skin and, when she finally fell asleep, her knees were bent tightly to her chest and one hand encircled her right foot.

CHAPTER THIRTEEN

HER FOOT WAS THE FIRST THING LILIHA THOUGHT OF THE next morning, and she ran all the way to Kalaupapa landing even though she knew she should walk slowly, step carefully. Her chest burned by the time she reached Martha's house. She smelled the smoke of a cooking fire, but saw no one. The door stood open and laughter floated from inside. There was no mistaking Hana's voice.

"It just had the most puzzled expression on its face," Hana was saying. "I've never seen a mouse with such a face. Almost like a person." Someone mumbled a reply. "Oh, I shooed it out. It ran to the wall and hid between the stones."

Liliha stepped through the doorway. "Hana?"

"Liliha!" Hana rocked forward across the room and closed her arms around the girl. "Ahia, look who's come to visit us!"

Ahia sat in a chair, a navy blue blanket wrapped around his shoulders. He nodded slowly, but his eyes seemed to stare right past her.

"Liliha, I haven't seen you in—how long do you suppose it's been?" Hana patted her shoulder. "I haven't been able to get to the hospital." Hana returned to the fire and bent over a thick black pot hung above the flames. "The soup is ready anytime you want to eat, Ahia. Are you hungry?"

Ahia didn't answer, didn't even seem to have heard the question.

"Why don't I go ahead and put some in a bowl for you, and you just eat what you want?" Hana ladled a generous amount of steaming broth into a bowl. She set the bowl and a spoon on the narrow table and helped Ahia shift his chair in front of it.

"Liliha? Would you like some?" Hana was already filling a second bowl. Liliha slid onto an empty chair. The seat bottom was flat and hard and pinched at her bones. The broth Hana set before her was thin, but smelled delicious. Hana fixed a third bowl and lowered herself onto a chair across from Liliha. Liliha had just begun to swipe her spoon into her bowl when she saw Hana bow her head. Ahia stared listlessly at his soup.

"Lord," Hana began, and Liliha hastily let go of her spoon, the handle clinking against the edge of the bowl. Hana's eyes were closed, her face peaceful. "We thank You for the nourishing food we eat today and for bringing our friend Liliha to visit us, and we thank You for our continued health and happiness."

Liliha glanced at Ahia. His skin was thin and dry; it pulled sharply against the bones of his face. His lips were dry, too, flecked with bits of dead skin, and he kept putting out his tongue and running it slowly across them. His tongue had a sore on it, near the tip, a white whorl set against the pink. She'd hoped he would be better, not only for Hana's sake but—

selfishly—so that it would be easier to ask Hana about the shoes. How could Hana think of anything or anyone else when Ahia was like this? Liliha stared down at her hands.

"Amen," Hana finished, picking up her spoon. Liliha echoed her, wondering what the word meant anyway. She'd heard the missionaries say it, too. Was it like saying good-bye to God?

When Liliha looked up again, Hana was watching her. "I haven't been to the hospital for a long time. It's terrible. Those poor people. Just when they start to get used to having someone to help them." She shook her head. "But I can't go there, not now."

Liliha glanced at Ahia, who didn't seem to have heard anything his wife said. With a blank, shuttered face, he stared at his soup.

"I'm sorry he's so sick," Liliha said.

"It's a fever. It gets a little better some days, but then terrible again."

Hana watched her husband with gentle eyes. She picked up his spoon and stirred it around in his bowl as if that might give him an appetite. His expression didn't change.

"Go on, Liliha," Hana said. "Eat."

It felt somehow wrong to eat when Ahia was so sick and Hana so troubled, but the soup, although thin and watery, was the best food Liliha had tasted since coming to Molokai. She tried to swallow silently and rubbed her right foot surreptitiously against the floor to test it. Still numb. She wondered, as she ate, how to bring up the subject of shoes.

While she was still trying to figure that out, Hana asked, "Have you been able to trade much lately?"

"I haven't had time for it."

Hana looked at her, puzzled.

"I'm building a hut," Liliha explained.

A smile started across Hana's face. "A hut?"

"So I won't have to live with Pauahi or with anybody else. I won't have to haul water for anyone or give them any of my food."

Something flickered deep in Hana's eyes. "It isn't *bad* to do those things."

"It is when the person squeezes every last drop of sweat out of you and then tries to pretend you should be grateful."

Hana nodded gravely. "Maybe it's a good thing, then, that you get away from Pauahi. But you might not want to forget her completely." Wood creaked as Hana settled back in her chair. "So, are you building this house by yourself?"

"Manukekua's been helping me," Liliha said casually. To her annoyance, her face burned hot at the words. She pressed her hands against her cheeks to cool them. And if that wasn't bad enough, Hana was grinning at her as if she knew exactly how much Liliha liked Manukekua.

"The Captain's boy? Hmm. Well, I'm glad you don't have to do the whole thing by yourself." Hana turned away. "Ahia? Are you all right?"

He'd begun to shiver almost convulsively, even with the blanket pulled around his shoulders. Hana helped him to a pile of mats.

"There now. You rest." Ahia turned his back to the room. Hana returned to the table and dropped into her chair, not picking up her spoon.

"Are you going to eat any more?" Liliha asked.

Hana shook her head absently. "I'm not hungry. But you go ahead."

Liliha finished her soup, trying not to show how she savored each spoonful. Hana patted her hand and said, "I like to go outside for a little while on such a beautiful day. What do you think?"

They walked a short distance from the house onto the rocky sand, Liliha taking small steps. She sat down with her knees inside the embrace of her arms. Hana stood beside her, hands on hips, legs apart, looking massive and strong, as if even the fiercest storm couldn't knock her down.

"It really is as beautiful as Oahu," Hana said, turning to look at the *pali* rearing up behind them. "More beautiful. But in a different way. Not so friendly, is it?"

"No," Liliha answered. "Not friendly." She imagined Uncle Malietoa's furious face. Oahu hadn't always been so friendly either.

Hana lowered herself onto the sand, her legs jutting straight out in front of her. She leaned back, her palms spread flat behind her to support her weight. She sighed. "I worry about Ahia. But you just have to trust in God."

Liliha dug a big toe in the sand. She didn't think she trusted much in *anybody*. Except her mother. Maybe Manukekua, if he could shake himself free of the Captain. And, in *some* ways, Hana.

"Here's the seaweed you needed," a dry, cool voice said from behind Liliha, who jumped, startled. The woman with the cluster of moles stopped beside Hana. "Solomon donated an old shirt to the cause." She handed a basket to Hana. The basket held a folded gray cotton shirt and thick green seaweed rolled into a ball bigger than Liliha's fist.

"Thank you, Martha," Hana said. "It will make a good poultice. If this doesn't bring the fever down . . ." She didn't finish.

Liliha looked at Martha's severe hair, her unsympathetic eyes, her hands, which were lean and tough from work. Those same hands had written letters. Liliha imagined asking Martha to write a letter for her, imagined trying to explain what she wanted it to say and why she wanted the letter in the first place. Would Martha keep secret what Liliha put in the letter? Or would she tell Hana of Liliha's plans so Hana could try to crush those hopes once and for all?

Martha *looked* like a person who could keep a secret.

"Oh," Hana said. "I'm sorry. Martha, you've never met my friend Liliha, have you?"

"I've seen her," Martha said, reaching to take the basket again. "I'll start the poultice." She turned away and went into the house.

"She really is a good woman," Hana said. "Just a bit . . . terse."

Liliha felt queasy at the thought of approaching Martha for help. She didn't think she could do it.

That meant she would just have to trust Hana, hope that Hana would help her no matter what Hana's own opinions were. Anyway, right now she had a more immediate concern.

"Hana," she said abruptly, "do you have a pair of shoes?"

Hana turned toward her. "Why do you want shoes?" Although her voice was kind, panic swelled in Liliha's chest. She couldn't bring herself to say the words out loud. That would make it all true. When Liliha didn't speak, Hana didn't ask again.

"I wore shoes when I lived in the city," Hana said. "Ahia liked to. I never did. But when I knew we were coming here, well, there didn't seem much point in holding on to all those clothes." Her face was sad. "I gave everything away except for a couple of dresses."

Unconsciously, Liliha reached down and rubbed her foot. She wished that Hana would volunteer something about Ahia's shoes. Liliha couldn't just ask to have them. That would be like blurting out that Ahia wouldn't be needing them anytime soon.

Hana's face had relaxed and her eyes were quiet as she watched an 'iwa, its feathers as dark as the sea, gliding high above the choppy water. "It *is* beautiful here, Liliha. Even the *pali* is beautiful."

"It's like a cage."

"But it's beautiful, too."

"Don't you ever get homesick, Hana?"

Hana closed her eyes briefly. "Yes and no. Yes, it can make me sad when I think about home, but then I think about how *this* is home now. And the whole of the earth is only home for a while anyway. It seems silly to worry too much about it."

"But, Hana, I want to go home. *Really* home."

"What about the hut you're building?"

"It could never be *home*."

Hana picked up a stone from the sand and rubbed it with one thumb. "Are you so sure?"

Was it sitting beside the ocean and looking out at the waves that aroused such furious discontent in Liliha? "I can't stay here forever, Hana. Not for the rest of my life."

"Liliha—"

"People might not suspect. Not if I kept my sleeves down," she said in a rush. "And wore shoes. And if I didn't let—"

"Liliha, you can't hide your illness from the world. Maybe for a few months, for a year or two, but not forever. And would you want that? To always have to hide?"

"Is it any worse than *this*?" Liliha spread her arms wide. "We're hiding here, too, aren't we? Only we didn't even get to make the choice. They told us we have to stay hidden. So no one has to see us or touch us or . . ." She broke off. "I don't want to stay here."

"You have to stay here." Hana's voice was matter-of-fact.

"I can't do it."

"You *must*."

"They could be wrong. Maybe I don't even have *ma'i pākē*."

"Liliha . . ." Hana touched her shoulder.

"Well, they could have made a mistake."

"Is there something wrong with your feet?"

"No!"

Hana was quiet for a moment. "Things don't just happen, Liliha. There's a reason you're here."

"To waste my life."

"No! God wouldn't do that."

Liliha felt Hana's hand tighten on her shoulder and she shrugged it away. Hana remained silent. What was it like to have the kind of belief Hana had?

As if she knew what Liliha thought, Hana said, "I wish someone had helped you know Christ before you came here. It would be a great comfort to you now to be able to trust." Hana's face was utterly placid.

Anger, shockingly strong, shook Liliha's voice. "How do *you* know what God is like, anyway?" Her hands clenched at the ground, digging below the surface to where the sand was cold and wet. She knew she shouldn't say anything more, but the words seemed to push their way out without warning. "What's Jesus, anyway? He died, just like"—she gasped, squirmed her dead foot against the wet sand—"just like I'm going to."

"Liliha—"

"What makes you think you know more than anyone else?"

"Liliha," Hana said in a still, hurt voice, but broke off when a shrill wail rose behind them. Hana was on her feet before Liliha could even look around. The cry came again, from Martha's house. It had to be Ahia.

Hana vanished through the doorway, pulling the door shut behind her. Liliha stepped uncertainly toward the house. There were more cries, muted now but edged with terror and mixed with hoarse sobs. Liliha's anger emptied itself, leaving a great hollow sack in her belly.

She stood outside the door for a long time until she could no longer hear Ahia, but only Hana's muffled voice; then she turned away and started toward the road.

She had no shoes, hadn't even had a chance—or the

courage—to ask about a letter. And now Hana would probably hate her, for arguing, for insulting Hana's god.

The wind gained strength and, when she finally stepped through the doorway of her half-finished house deep in the shadow of the *pali,* Liliha thought she'd never heard a wind sound so lonesome.

Chapter Fourteen

She dreamed that her toes fell off, one at a time, then her fingers. The nightmare jerked Liliha out of an exhausted sleep at dawn. She clutched her knees to her chest and rocked silently. Terrible images rose in her mind: the man in the hospital; Ahia curled on his mat, shrieking. Her face burned when she remembered what she'd said to Hana.

"But what about what she said to me?" Liliha muttered to herself. Her chest ached. "Oh, Hana."

She still didn't know where she would find *real* shoes, but in the meantime she could make herself a pair of sandals. She had made sandals for Grandmother. Near her hut, where the elevation was still low and the ground moist, *kī* grew abundantly, some of the plants taller than Liliha's head, shiny green leaves spiraling around thick yellow stems. She crossed to one of the plants now, pulled loose a handful of leaves, and bit out the midrib that ran down the center of each one. Of course, to make anything properly—from mats to shoes—the leaves should be left to dry to a dull brown, suitable for weaving strong, braided cords. Liliha didn't know how the cords, and the sandals made from them, would turn out if she used fresh leaves. Shrugging, she tugged another handful from the plant. Any sandals would be better than nothing.

Liliha counted her bundle of leaves. Fifty. That might be enough. Since they hadn't been dried, there was no need to soak them in water to soften them. She sat down and began to work with such concentration that she saw nothing except the glossy surface of the leaves. She braided until she had two cords, each about six feet long. She laid each rope in a U shape, making sure the open space at the center was as wide as her foot. Then she began to weave and knot the remaining, flat leaves across the frames formed by those cords.

She still hadn't finished by late morning when Manukekua crouched beside her. He glanced at the hut.

"No," Liliha said. "I haven't done any more work on it."

Manukekua pointed at the sandals as Liliha wove another leaf across the sole. "What's that?" he asked.

"I'm making sandals."

"Liliha?"

She shook her head. She couldn't look up, couldn't look at anything, and then tears ran down her cheeks.

"Liliha." Manukekua kneeled in front of her. He grasped her shoulders and gently shook her. "Liliha? What is it?" Her throat was so clogged with tears that she couldn't answer, but she didn't need to. Manukekua guessed. "What's wrong with your feet?"

Liliha drew in her breath with a painful hiss. "Nothing's wrong."

"Liliha. You don't wear shoes. You've never said a word

about wishing you had shoes. And your feet are too tough to need them. I know. I've seen you walk over rocks and shells and you were just fine. And now you're making sandals instead of finishing the hut?"

Liliha exhaled long and slow.

"So?" Manukekua said, leaning forward. "What's wrong? Does your foot hurt?"

"It *doesn't* hurt."

He understood immediately. "You can't feel it?"

She reached down and touched the sole of her right foot. "It's numb. All this part, here."

Manukekua bent down to examine the skin. His eyebrows clenched together as if he saw something terrible.

"What?" Liliha asked, grasping at him. "What?"

"I've never seen so much dirt in my life. No wonder you want shoes."

She pushed at him, laughing despite herself. Manukekua gently touched the ball of her foot.

"Well, I really *can't* see anything through the dirt," he said. "But shoes might be a good idea, so you don't end up cutting your foot open and not even knowing it until it's . . ." He stopped.

"Too late?"

He bowed his head.

"Why don't they give people shoes when they come here, anyway?" Liliha complained.

"They never give out much clothing, and that's only once a year. And anyway, shoes? I don't think shoes are usually part of the ration."

"I asked Hana if she had any," Liliha said quietly.

"She said no?" But Liliha didn't want to talk about Hana.

"She said no."

"But you'll have these at least," Manukekua said, nodding at the unfinished sandals.

Liliha sagged. "I need shoes that are strong. That nothing can cut through." But what could she do? Hope that when they eventually handed out the clothing rations, they might be extravagant and include shoes with her portion? And what would her feet look like by then? Liliha beat her fist into the earth. "I went in the hospital," she said. "There was a man there. Oh, Manukekua—his legs . . . they were . . ." She couldn't finish.

Manukekua touched her arm, then picked up an unfinished shingle of grass and began to knot more blades into the mass. "There might be a way," he said. Liliha raised her head. "On the other side of the *pali*, topside, there are some villages. People trade. They get things from the other islands."

Liliha nodded. "Hana told me people sometimes come down the *pali*."

"Well, people sometimes go *up* it, too."

She turned her head and stared at the cliff, her eye measuring the height and the steepness. What would it be like to stand at the very top, looking down at Kalaupapa? How free would she feel? She'd thought about it before, of course, thought of climbing up the *pali* and vanishing over the top of it. Who would miss her?

"You've gone over?" she asked.

"Yes."

"How many times have you been over?"

"Only a couple. When the Captain needed liquor really bad and the supplies the sailor was supposed to bring were late. I've only been to one of the villages."

Liliha grabbed his arm. "What's it like?"

"They have a market, fishing, plenty of trade. People come there from other villages topside."

"Do they call you a leper? Or chase you away?"

"No. A couple of them wouldn't talk to me. But most of them do." He reached up, touched the edge of the sore on his face. "Maybe a lot of them don't know what this means. And the lepers here who really look like lepers are too sick to cross the *pali* anyway."

Liliha thought. "Do you know if I could find shoes?"

"I've seen people trade them. And, Liliha—I've seen people use money there, too. Not everybody, but some."

Liliha's fingers tightened around his arm. "When can we go?"

Manukekua gently worked his arm free. "It's a hard climb, Liliha, and then it's a long walk to the south shore of the island. Most of the villages are all the way on the opposite side of Molokai from here. It's a good ten miles at least once you're over the *pali.*"

"But you've gone. Other people have gone."

"Not many. It's too hard a trip once you really start to get sick. I thought I could take some of your carvings with me and sell them for you. You said that you needed money. I wanted to do that for you. I could try to bring back money *and* shoes."

"I want to go," Liliha insisted.

"We'd be gone a couple of days."

"What about the Captain? How will you be able to—?"

Manukekua's eyes sharpened. "He's getting low on whiskey and rum. If I make sure his stash goes down and hide any new bottles that come with the supplies, he'll be ordering me to get over that *pali* and find more fast. But what about you? How much do you have to trade?"

"Not much. I've been working on the hut and now the sandals. Shoes will be expensive, won't they? I'll need to have a lot of things ready to trade." She hated having to use any of the carvings to get shoes. She'd rather sell them all for the money she'd need to bribe a sailor to get a letter to her mother.

Manukekua paused, thinking. "What if I work on the hut so you can start carving?"

Liliha raised her hands in protest. "But you shouldn't have to do all the work when it's my—"

His hands closed over hers, curling her fingers into her palms. "That's why I want to, Liliha. *Because* it's yours." His fingers tightened, then drew away. "I'll come whenever I can and I'll work as long as I can. That hut will be finished before we leave. I promise."

Liliha ducked her head. Her terror about her feet eased a little. Manukekua always seemed to be able to make her feel better. "Thank you." She looked up at him with mock seriousness. "As long as you've learned to knot the *pili* hard enough. I want this hut to be *strong.*"

"By the time I'm done, nobody in the world will be better at building grass huts. People in Honolulu will want to burn down all their wood houses and hire me to put up *pili* instead."

"So I should *really* be grateful." She smiled.

"You should." His eyes caught hers.

Feathers brushed deep within Liliha's stomach. "I am, you know," she said quietly. "Grateful." Manukekua just nodded and, picking up the grass bundle, began working on it again.

After that, he came whenever he could, which was usually every two or three days. As he became more practiced, the shingles he wove and lashed to the framework grew sturdier, more shapely. He worked on the roof first, finished it, and moved on to the walls. Liliha sat cross-legged on the ground, her head bent close to the knife as she peeled away thin slices from each scrap of wood. Occasionally she scraped the edge of the blade against a flat stone to sharpen it. Although she and Manukekua didn't speak much, she liked to see him when she glanced up from her work and liked to hear the rustle of dry grass as he tied the shingles into place. She would be glad when the hut was finished and the rain couldn't get to her anymore.

Once, on her way to fetch water, she saw Kalani. They were both walking the same direction on the path, but Liliha was a good distance behind Kalani. Liliha immediately slipped into the brush growing beside the trail and crouched there, watching as Kalani moved farther away. Opuhumanuu was with her, swinging a pair of buckets that must have been empty. Kalani was shouting at her about something and Opuhumanuu stumbled along with her shoulders cringing forward and her head low. Even from a distance, Liliha could see that Kalani's hair had grown longer. It was at least an inch long now, maybe two, and it clung, matted, to her scalp. There was something strange about the way Kalani walked. Was that a slight limp, a vague hitch with each step taken by the left leg?

Her voice sounded the same as it rose in a torrent of curses at Opuhumanuu's stupidity, her clumsy uselessness.

Liliha watched until they'd moved out of sight, then she clambered out of the weeds and hurried back to her hut. She went thirsty that day, and the next, until Manukekua offered to fetch the water for her. She let him do it that first time, grateful that he never asked where she found the bucket.

In the next few weeks, she avoided the hospital compound and fetched water only when Manukekua couldn't. Manukekua picked up her rations for her so she wouldn't have to risk Kalani's fury. She wondered if Kalani ever forgot a grudge. That didn't seem likely.

She spent almost all her time carving. Sometimes, as she carved, Liliha thought about going to see Hana. She was afraid to see her again. What if Hana hated her now? She tried to tell herself she didn't care if she saw Hana or not. What did Hana talk about anyway, but God and love, love and God? What did any of that have to do with this place? But then the anger would vanish and Liliha would miss Hana with some of the same pain with which she missed her own mother.

In any case, she would *have* to work up the courage to go back to Hana once she had money in hand. At least, she had to if she wanted that letter.

Liliha didn't know how many carvings she would need to trade for a pair of shoes. And what sort of money would the carvings be worth? She was glad the Scottish doctor had shown her bills and shiny coins and tried to explain to her how many of one kind of coin equaled a different size coin or a paper bill. She just wished that she'd paid more attention and understood it better.

She dug a deep hole behind her hut, and as soon as she finished a carving, she placed it in the hole for safekeeping and covered the opening with vines. Sometimes, when he had time, Manukekua scoured the peninsula for more remnants of wood for her. He tore planks from the fence surrounding the compound and brought those to her. Other days, frustrated with having no more wood, Liliha ventured cautiously out herself. The hole gradually filled with bowls and plates, combs and elaborate stamps for inking designs onto cloth.

At least when she carved she could forget about her feet for a few minutes. Despite the rudimentary sandals she wore day and night, the numbness spread through the entire right foot and up the ankle and began to afflict the left foot as well. It was much more pleasant to concentrate on perfecting the talons of a *pueo,* a Hawaiian owl, cut into the side of a cup.

After a month, an afternoon came when the last wall needed only one more shingle. Manukekua handed the bundle to Liliha and she positioned it on the frame. Stepping back, she examined the wall and nodded. The shingles were thick and set tightly against each other. They would keep out rain. She pressed her face into the grass. It was scratchy and the dust made her nose twitch, but it smelled clean and strong. She whirled toward Manukekua with a brilliant grin. Darting forward, she clasped his hands, then pulled away and circled the hut twice, staring at it, her arms gripped hard across her chest.

Manukekua waited for her beside the door. "It's a good hut, Liliha."

She couldn't stop grinning. "It's not as comfortable as the Captain's, I know, but—"

"But it's *yours*," Manukekua finished. For a second, she thought she saw envy flicker across his face. "So," he continued, "tonight I pour out the rest of the rum. There isn't much left anyway. The Captain's already nervous because the whiskey's gone. He'll be ordering me topside any day."

"I'll be ready."

Manukekua hunched his shoulders and cleared his throat. "Are you *sure* you want to go?"

"Yes."

"It's just—it's a hard climb, and even after we get over the *pali* we have a long way to go, and with your feet . . ."

She leveled her eyes on him. "My feet will be all right."

"Are you—?"

"I'm going."

"Because I could take your carvings and trade them for you, so you—"

"I'm going."

He nodded. "Bring some rations, dried beef or salmon, nothing that needs to be cooked."

The night before they left, Liliha kneeled beside the hole behind her hut and pulled out the carvings. She pushed them into her sack.

Picking up the bucket, she drank the last water from it. She put her extra set of clothes into the bucket, then her comb, a small bag of rice, a half block of *pa'i 'ai*, a ribbon. Finally, she pressed her cheek against the pink shawl and placed the shawl on top of the other objects in the bucket. The pale pink lace gleamed faintly in the moonlight. She lowered the bucket into the hole, covered the hole with vines and, sack in tow, crept inside the hut to wait for dawn and Manukekua.

CHAPTER FIFTEEN

"It's going to be steep in spots," Manukekua said over his shoulder. "But not too bad yet. Just don't push hard at the beginning or you'll be worn out before we're halfway up."

The blue shadows of early morning obscured his face. Despite the near darkness, he moved without hesitation, carrying Liliha's sack along with his own empty one.

Another fifty paces and the path sloped suddenly upward, then became almost level again. Plants began to crowd more thickly around it. In the slowly gathering light, Liliha could make out the long stems of sword ferns. She breathed in the rich smell of moisture, earth, and vegetation. Already the waterfalls were louder. Crooked as an old woman's finger, the path curved back and forth. Liliha's breath shortened; her muscles strained. Her right foot was a stone and her left not much better.

When she looked down, she was astonished to see how high they'd already climbed. The peninsula stretched, shorn and dull, to a dark blue smear of ocean. The crater was a black circle ringed with green at the center of the land.

Manukekua wiped his face on the bottom of his shirt. "See that waterfall up there?" Liliha twisted to follow his pointing arm. "We can eat once we reach it. It's not good to eat the beef unless you have water handy."

The path was exhausting. A series of switchbacks kept the trail from being impossibly steep, but it seemed to go on forever. Sweat poured down Liliha's back. Her shirt was tight and hot and she unfastened the small buttons at the neck and rolled the sleeves past her elbows. Climbing had loosened her sandals, worn thin red grooves around her ankles and over the tops of her feet where she'd lashed them in place that morning.

The waterfall was very loud now, off somewhere to the left. Occasional cool drops drizzled against Liliha's arms. A boulder loomed in front of her, the rough gray rock freckled with water. Manukekua had already climbed onto it and he reached down to help Liliha scrabble up beside him. A fine mist cooled her face. Manukekua pointed. "Now we can drink."

On the boulder's far side, water fell away, sheer as a veil, into the air. Manukekua stretched one of Liliha's bowls into the plunging water. He passed the bowl to Liliha. The water tasted pure and delicious. When she was done, Manukekua drank, then splashed water over his head until his hair was soaked and flat against his neck and his shirt was streaked.

Liliha brought out her dried beef, and they each chewed strips of the meat. Liliha craned her neck back to look up at the *pali*. She felt like she'd been climbing it her entire life.

"You'll really start to feel the wind when we get closer to the top," Manukekua warned. "There's no protection at all up there."

Liliha was thirsty again almost as soon as they resumed climbing. Her legs moved mechanically. She made the mistake, once, of looking down. The *pali* seemed to collapse into empty space. The vision left her dizzy.

The trees thinned out, became tenaciously crooked, clutching at the slope with knotted roots. Wind plunged between the branches as if it wanted to strip away every piece of bark, every leaf. The wind beat at Liliha's back and tore at her hair. Manukekua turned to her. "Liliha!" he shouted. "We made it!" He caught one arm around her shoulders and turned her in the direction they'd come from. The wind ripped his voice away. "Look!" He held her shoulders with both hands, steadying her.

Wind flapped at Liliha's hair and skirt. The sweat on her back evaporated and the fabric of her shirt snapped dry. She raised her palms, letting the air rush through the spaces between her fingers. In the distance, the ocean suddenly glinted as if a thousand dolphins leaped from the water and plunged back into it. Hana was right. Kalaupapa was beautiful.

Pulling away from Manukekua, Liliha strode to the edge of the *pali* and leaned forward into the perfect, pure air. Her head was clear, as clear as the air and the view. When she finally turned back to Manukekua, his eyes were bright. "I wanted it to surprise you," he said. "This is my favorite place."

It was hard to leave that view, but the rest of Molokai waited for them. As they left the *pali* behind, Liliha thought that the area seemed strangely lonely. She looked for villages or settlers, but saw none.

As she and Manukekua walked south, they gradually descended to a plain where Liliha finally saw houses, only a few, but much neater and more prosperous than anything at Kalaupapa. Some were constructed of wood, others of tidy grass, and still others combined both materials. Gardens surrounded them, and cultivated fields of *taro*, sugarcane, and coconut.

Manukekua turned onto a narrow trail heading southeast. Peaks of hills jagged up ahead of them now.

"I thought we were done climbing," Liliha said, dismayed.

Manukekua nodded. "There are trails that cut through the valleys. We won't have to climb much."

"What's that one?" Liliha pointed at the tallest peak.

"Kamakou."

"Why haven't we passed any villages yet?"

"It's just farmers here. The villages are on the shore."

They took a long break in the afternoon to eat more dried beef and breadfruit that Manukekua had brought, and stopped a second time to let Liliha rest her feet. It was early evening when they left the low plains behind and headed into the valley between two hills. Thick clusters of *painiu* grew around the mossy trunks, the waxy leaves glowing pale silver in the filtered sunlight. Manukekua crouched to pull apart the *painiu*'s slender, upright leaves so Liliha could see the water collected in the reservoir at the base. "You never have to worry about being thirsty here," he said. "It's like a cup." He stood. "We should stop soon." He glanced at Liliha's feet.

"I can keep walking. How long?"

Manukekua narrowed his eyes at the long purple shadows enveloping the path. "If we only stop to rest once or twice, it'll be dark."

"We were practically in the dark this morning and we were going up a cliff." When Manukekua didn't answer, Liliha pushed past him. Her right foot stumped like a club and her legs were so tired that she was amazed she could still force them forward. She used to be able to walk all day without feeling tired.

The sky was a soft black. As the land flattened toward the ocean, the path became a genuine road, houses scattered alongside it. Liliha smelled smoke and fish steaming.

"Were you by yourself the first time you came here?" Liliha asked.

"I followed a minister who comes to Kalaupapa sometimes. I'd heard that he was visiting and I found out when he was going to leave. The good thing is that he didn't stay around Kalaupapa too long. If I'd had to wait for him to leave, the Captain would have been impatient for his whiskey. Furious. I was lucky."

"Did the minister see you?"

"Sure. But he let me follow. He even left food for me a couple of times after he'd stopped to rest." Liliha could barely see Manukekua's arm pointing to a dark space behind several houses. "They grow guava in those fields. And sweet potatoes. At least, they did the last time I was here."

Salt tanged the air. To Liliha's right, she saw dark waves rushing and retreating. A ragged line of canoes was scattered along the beach, well above the tide line.

"There," Manukekua said, stopping.

The houses of the village, lit with candles and oil lamps, glowed in the distance like luminous fish motionless at night just beneath the water's surface. The silhouettes of palm trees bent protectively over the buildings.

"There are fishponds all along the shore here," Manukekua noted. "They fatten up fish in them." Liliha nodded. She'd seen fishponds before, built of coral and basalt, prisons for the unfortunate saltwater fish trapped within them. "The market is down there." Manukekua pointed along the road. "But not till morning. There's nothing to do now."

"Except sleep."

Too tired to be hungry or even very curious, Liliha dropped gratefully onto the sand while Manukekua sank down a few feet away. She pressed one side of her face into the sand, thinking how cool and fine it was, just like the sand at home.

CHAPTER SIXTEEN

A CLATTER OF WOOD SHOOK LILIHA AWAKE. SHE SAT UP, confused. Manukekua was still asleep, curled into a tight ball beside her, his arms bent around his head. He looked like he was trying to protect himself from a beating. Liliha watched him with a sudden, sharp sympathy until another clatter drew her attention to the road, where a woman pushed a handcart. Splinters stuck out from the spokes like bits of unruly hair; the wheels wobbled and groaned. Dawn moved ghostly gray through the sky.

Liliha climbed stiffly to her knees. Was there any part of her body that wasn't sore? When she reached up to touch her hair, her arms and shoulders burned like white fire.

The cart lurched through a rut with an enormous rattle that woke Manukekua.

"They're coming," he said, clambering to his feet.

Liliha's stomach yawned. She wondered what foods the villagers would sell. Anything but dried beef.

As they approached, the village was already bustling with people setting out guavas and rice, shaking mats clean, dragging canoes to the water. A dog, small and lean with coarse yellow hair, ran out from behind a house and darted at Liliha's feet. When she kneeled down, the dog let her stroke its fur.

"Oh, Manukekua." Liliha smiled up at him and ruffled the dog's ears.

"It must belong to somebody here," he said, not bending down.

"Don't you want to pet him?"

"No. Then I'd just want to take him back with us." The dog yapped once and trotted away, disappearing past a display of baskets brimming with coconuts, *kukui* nuts, and shark meat.

"The fishing must be good here," Liliha said. She stepped forward to touch a net spread across a stone wall in front of a hut. The net was made of *olona*, finely woven, and had a wooden ring at one end. Liliha remembered nets like this from home. The wooden hoop held the net's mouth open so that it easily swallowed masses of *manini* and eels, which were good to eat, and fantailed *'o'ili*, which were not. She thought of the few meager fish she'd caught with Pauahi's net and envied the villagers. Could she buy such a net—so finely meshed—or make one? She looked at the water. The surf was gentle, the shoreline clean. The villagers would have no trouble wading out into the sea. It was nothing like Kalaupapa's turbulent, rock-strewn surf.

"Think how easy it would be to land rations here," she said. "They should have had us live here, not Kalaupapa."

Manukekua shook his head. "It's too easy for people to come and go. They wanted a place where we'd be left alone."

They walked on. Liliha just wanted to look and look. The air shimmered with talk and snatches of song. People smiled at each other and gossiped, made jokes and laughed. She watched women wander from one trader to another, purchasing coconut pudding and *leis,* inspecting beads and breadfruit with critical eyes. Children meandered through. People wore colorful mixtures of Hawaiian and *haole* clothing: blouses tucked into long skirts; simple loose dresses of delicate cloth made from the white-flowering branches of the *pū hala.* It amazed Liliha to think that this village existed on the same island as Kalawao.

At one makeshift stall, she saw a woman with a face as shrunken and tight as leather selling bright baskets of fruits and vegetables. Above the baskets, on cords strung between tree trunks, clothing fluttered: cotton skirts, canvas dungarees, *kī* capes. Liliha glimpsed the pointed toes of a pair of black shoes nearly hidden by a basket of sweet potatoes. Behind the basket, she found even more shoes. Liliha pulled them out, one pair at a time.

She jabbed at Manukekua with one shoe's thin, high heel. "Can you see me heading off to Wai'ale'ia to fetch water in these?" she said, laughing. Other shoes were better. Liliha liked the soft leather pair that resembled moccasins, but she prodded at the pliable soles. "Do you think they'll protect my feet?" she asked, squinting at Manukekua.

He took one of the shoes from her and flexed it. "Maybe not as much as you want."

She decided on a pair of sturdy, low boots with buttons that curved up to the ankle. The leather-faced woman haggled over the price for a long time, rubbing a forefinger along the edge of her single front tooth as she considered each offer. In the end, she took more than half the carvings—and the finest, as well—

in Liliha's sack. Liliha, not sure if she'd made a respectable deal or been cheated, clutched the shoes against her chest.

"What about—?" Manukekua looked uncomfortable.

"What?"

"Don't you need stockings, too?" He blushed.

"I don't have any," the leather-faced woman interjected.

"Maybe somebody else?" Manukekua suggested.

Liliha raised her sack, felt how light it was. If she wanted to have any money to offer a sailor to carry a message to her mother, if she wanted to buy a better net, she couldn't afford to waste any of her carvings bargaining for unnecessary items.

"They'll be all right," she told Manukekua, and hurried to the water. She tore off the sandals, rinsed her feet in the low waves, then sat down, raising her feet in the air and wiggling her toes until they were dry.

She slid her feet into the boots, hooked the buttons with awkward, infuriating slowness, and clomped across the beach to where Manukekua waited for her.

"How are they?" he asked, and broke into a grin as Liliha tottered back and forth in front of him.

"Are they supposed to feel strange?"

"I guess so, if you're not used to them."

"It's like my feet can't feel *anything* now." Her ankles were stiff, as if gripped by hands. It was nothing like wearing the sandals.

"Do they hurt?"

She considered. "It's not that. They just—it's hard to walk." She lumbered several more steps. "I'll get used to them."

Manukekua watched her dubiously. She poked at her sack. "Where do you think is a good place to set up?"

She didn't need much space to lay out the carvings that remained. She found an empty patch beside a woman selling brilliantly dyed cloth and spread out bowls, cups, spoons and combs.

"I'll come find you when I'm done," said Manukekua. He slipped easily among the milling villagers. Liliha watched him go until a man stopped in front of her, picked up a bowl, and pretended to drink from it. He held the bowl near his face and turned it around and around.

"What will you take for it?" he asked.

The carvings sold steadily. Liliha demanded cash at first, trying to sound confident, like she knew all about money. She bargained down to food or cloth or sewing needles only if she truly believed the person had no money. Many of them didn't. By late morning, she had a small stash of bananas and mangoes, but less money than she'd hoped. *If* she was even counting it correctly. Would she have enough to get a letter to her mother? Would it be enough to bring her mother secretly to Kalaupapa and for Liliha to bribe someone to let them steal back to Oahu on a ship?

It would *have* to be enough.

Liliha tilted her head back and closed her eyes with a sigh. Voices chattered, bright bird calls. People were *alive* here. Even the land glittered and pulsed, nothing like the bare, swept peninsula where lepers waited to die.

A mother walked by, her baby squirming in her arms. The

woman smiled at Liliha, a smile so warm and immediate that it poured through Liliha like sunlight. Liliha grinned back.

What would it be like to live in the house next to that woman? To gossip with her about the other villagers in the morning and play games with the baby and not once during the entire day think about disease or fear or death? Liliha grinned, just thinking about it.

When Manukekua returned later that day, the canvas bag slung over his shoulder looked heavy. Liliha heard bottles clink.

"You sold a lot," he observed, watching Liliha push the few remaining carvings into her sack.

"Did you get enough whiskey?"

"Whiskey and rum, and lots of it."

On the way back, Manukekua tried to set a brisk pace, but had to keep stopping to wait for Liliha, who lingered in front of the different stands and displays. He was patient; he didn't call back to her or tell her to hurry. He just waited, watching her with a smile that made Liliha feel strangely shy, made her duck away again.

She traded for a net with such a fine mesh that even the puniest fish wouldn't escape. As she turned away from the stall, she saw a plain gold cross on a delicate chain. Liliha held the necklace against her palm. The cross was polished so that it glinted as she turned it in the sunlight. Would Hana think it was beautiful? Liliha might not ever agree with Hana about God or about staying at Kalaupapa until she died, but she missed Hana nevertheless. She wondered how sick Ahia was now. Maybe the necklace would make Hana feel a little better.

Jewelry was about as useless as her shawl, but she didn't care. She traded for it anyway. She tramped back to Manukekua, who helped her fasten the clasp around her neck so she wouldn't lose the necklace.

"It's for Hana," Liliha said, fingering the strange shape against her throat.

They passed the display where she'd bought her shoes, and Liliha nodded at the leathery woman. What would it be like to live in this village, setting out a display of her carvings right next to this woman? Was that really so impossible?

"Girl!" Liliha glanced over. The leather-faced woman stood at the edge of the road and looped one scrawny arm through the air. "Come here."

Stepping carefully in the new shoes, Liliha walked over to the woman, who drew her to the back of the display. The woman stared at Liliha with a grim mouth, and Liliha stopped smiling. Her stomach tightened as the woman pulled out a small wooden box and pushed back the hinged lid. Inside were cloth pouches and glass bottles.

The woman held a bottle in front of Liliha. *"Pawale,"* she said. "Mixed with *'awa.* And secret ingredients. Good for ailments of the skin. I've seen it cure leprosy." Liliha's heart squeezed in on itself. "I make medicines," the woman added. "I've helped many people."

Liliha drew back. She hugged her arms around herself and shook her head. "I don't have leprosy."

The woman's eyes pierced her. "I know these things."

"Well, you're wrong."

"I'm not blind. I saw how you were walking. I saw your

hands." She nodded at the discolored patches that spread from Liliha's wrists to her knuckles. "This will help you. Take it." The woman pushed the bottle into Liliha's sack. Liliha turned and fled, her shoes so heavy and stiff that she could hardly run.

"What did she want?" Manukekua asked, but Liliha shoved past him. Her face felt like it was about to fly apart in a dozen pieces. "Liliha!"

She stopped to plunge a hand into her sack. Her fingers closed on the bottle and drew it out. "This. She wanted to give me this."

Manukekua took it from her, turning the bottle from side to side. "What is it?"

"Medicine," Liliha said bitterly. She surged ahead, her shoes pounding the ground at each step. Manukekua, lugging the liquor bottles, struggled to catch up.

"Medicine for what?"

"What do you think?" She glanced back at him. "Leprosy. That's what we have, isn't it? That's what we are."

They walked in silence after that. As Liliha's anger burned down, her pace slackened. At first the shoes seemed awkward and clumsy, but they didn't hurt. As they continued to rub, the skin at the back of her left ankle began to sting. After a while, it felt like it was tearing open. The skin on her right ankle was too numb to register any pain. Liliha refused to put on her sandals again, not after what she'd gone through to get the shoes.

They stopped once in the late afternoon to eat and rest, then trudged on, even after darkness fell. The temperature sank and Liliha's clothes, damp with perspiration, grew chilly. The last solitary houses were behind them when they halted in a field for the night. They sat next to each other on the ground. Liliha eased the shoes off, trying not to press the leather against her blisters.

"Here." Manukekua put a piece of shark meat in her hand. She chewed mechanically, too exhausted to appreciate the delicious taste.

When they'd finished eating, Manukekua reached into his sack. He pulled out a small bowl tightly covered with leaves lashed into place with a narrow cord. He pressed it into Liliha's hands.

"What is it?"

"Coconut pudding. You said that was your favorite."

"Oh, Manukekua. Thank you."

"Do you have any spoons left?"

"One." She pillaged her sack. "We'll share it." She held the spoon out to him, but Manukekua said, "No, you take the first bite."

She savored the coconut, letting it rest sweet and thick on her tongue. She passed the bowl and spoon to Manukekua.

When they'd scraped the last of the pudding from the bowl, Liliha leaned back on her elbows. She thought about her mother making coconut pudding.

"Thank you, Manukekua," she said.

He lay back. Liliha could see that his eyes were open, staring at the sky. "I'm sorry that woman upset you," he said. "Giving you the medicine."

Liliha plucked at the grass in front of her. She opened her hands, letting the broken pieces flutter to the ground. "I was happy. I almost believed I could climb back over the *pali* and live with those people. And when she *saw* the leprosy . . . If I tried to live there, everybody would notice it. They'd make me leave."

Manukekua finally answered. "They might."

"So . . . if I ever escape from Kalaupapa, I'll be alone. I'll have to live away from people." She inched closer to him. Her voice wound tight. "But I'm going to get back to Oahu. You could come with me. There are forests where we can hide. My mother would be the only person who'd know we were there. She'd help us. I know she would."

"Liliha." Manukekua sat up. "You can't go back to Oahu."

"Don't you want to go back?"

"Liliha, I'm not leaving."

"Because of the Captain?" Her voice twisted. "Is he so wonderful?"

Manukekua flung his hands out. "Because there's no other place to go. Don't you understand? There's nowhere else to go."

"You just don't want to leave the Captain. Who's drunk all the time. Who treats you like his servant." She turned away, drew her knees to her chest, and rested her cheek against them.

"There's only one reason I can think of for you to run away," Manukekua said.

"What?"

"Kalani."

"If I leave Kalaupapa—" Liliha stopped and squared her shoulders. "*When* I leave Kalaupapa, I'll go because I want to.

And when I want to. Not because I'm running away from Kalani."

"Liliha—"

"No. I let Uncle Malietoa order me around, and my grandmother, too. But not Kalani. I'm through hiding from her." Liliha touched the knife blade through the fabric of her skirt. "And I *will* leave," she insisted. "I *am* going to get a message to my mother. And if I can't go there yet, then I want her to come here so I can talk to her. If she could see what Kalaupapa's really like, she'd *want* to help me get away."

Manukekua didn't move or speak.

"I need to talk to her. I need to *see* her."

Manukekua's voice was gentle. "Liliha. She could have been here with you all this time if she'd wanted to. She could have come as a *kōkua*."

Liliha's body stiffened. "No. She had to stay for my brother."

"Is he younger than you?"

"No," she answered reluctantly. "He's older." She didn't add that he was old enough that he was already married.

"She could have left him and come with you. Liliha—"

"She couldn't give up her whole life like that."

"Other people do."

"You don't know her."

He tilted his head to one side, listening.

"You don't know what things have been like for her. After my father died . . ." She hesitated. "He was out fishing when a storm hit. They didn't find his body for three days. When we moved in with my uncle, he never said a single kind word to any of us. He didn't care that his brother was dead. The only thing he was glad about was he could make me be Grandmother's servant. He didn't want to go near her. He was afraid he'd end up a leper."

"So he made you do it instead."

"Made me live with her. Eat with her. Comb her hair. Wash her clothes. Just so if anybody was in danger, it wouldn't be him or his own precious daughter."

"And your mother? Why didn't she stop him?"

Liliha turned on him with fierce eyes. "She *couldn't*. What was she supposed to do?"

"Would you have starved? Couldn't you and your mother and your brother have fished and found enough food without your uncle? Built a hut, like you just did?"

"My father had just died," Liliha said, anguished. "What was she supposed to do? What was *I* supposed to do?"

Manukekua reached for her hand, but Liliha shook him off. "Liliha, I just don't want you to be disappointed. About her coming here."

"I *won't* be. She'll come if she knows I really need her."

His hands floated uselessly. "Liliha, you can't expect she'll even get your message. And then for her to find a way here, to sneak onto Kalaupapa?"

Her hands were fists. The cool night air suddenly seemed hot, suffocating. Manukekua's words pushed at her, dark walls that threatened to cut her off from escape and from her mother as effectively as the *pali* separated lepers from the world. "Just because you're ready to give up doesn't mean I am," she said.

"Maybe you don't mind wasting the rest of your life, *dying* here, but I do. She'll come."

Her legs tensed with a desperate urge to run. Where? She touched the cross at her throat. What would she do if Hana refused to help her with the letter?

The sore under Manukekua's eye seemed to glow in the starlight. "Liliha, I'm not trying to hurt you."

She stared past him until he turned away from her. She stared at the sharp line where the land ended against the sky. Past that line, the cliff plummeted toward Kalaupapa and lepers dying in tumbledown huts or rotting on the hospital floor.

Liliha fingered the coins in her pocket and thought about what to say in the letter.

CHAPTER SEVENTEEN

THEY ARRIVED AT LILIHA'S HUT LATE THE NEXT MORNING after the long descent down the *pali*. Manukekua tried to say good-bye. Liliha ignored him. After he'd gone, she pulled off her shoes. The skin at the back of each ankle hung in a little flap over a raw pink blister. Tears swam in her eyes. She picked up the bottle of medicine and wrested the cork free. She tipped the bottle into her palm. The medicine was dark and oily, with black bits in it that looked like the grit and char left behind after a fire burns out. She sniffed it. It smelled vaguely of leaves and smoke.

Would the medicine really help? If it was a cure, why didn't the doctor at Kalihi Hospital back on Oahu use it? But maybe he hadn't even tried it, didn't give it a second thought because it wasn't *haole* medicine. She rubbed the ointment into her toes, her heels, the sores where the shoes rubbed, working it deeply into the skin. For a moment, she thought that the skin felt hot, but she might have imagined that. The heat vanished. She pushed the cork back into the bottle and went outside carrying the few utensils and combs that had gone unsold.

When she saw the secret hole she'd dug behind the house, Liliha stopped dead. The vines and leaves covering it had been moved. Not just by wind, but by something—or someone—insistent. The leaves had been knocked away, the vines torn.

An animal?

Or a person?

Liliha plunged forward and ripped the vines clear. She sank back on her heels, gasping in dismay. The bucket was still there and the few remnants of food she'd tucked inside it. But her mother's pink shawl was gone.

Liliha fumbled inside the bucket, hoping that somehow the shawl would reappear. She pulled out each item she'd stored in the hole and froze when her fingers closed on the polished handle of a wooden spoon. The spoon's handle was shaped like a joyous dolphin. Liliha dropped the spoon, letting it clatter against the bottom of the bucket.

It was the spoon that Kalani had stolen from Pauahi's house. Kalani hadn't left it here as some sort of exchange for the shawl, but as a sign. A sign that she knew where Liliha lived. Knew where she kept her supplies, her treasures. Knew *everything.*

Liliha stared into the surrounding trees. Kalani could be crouched, hiding, anywhere.

With a club. With a knife to slice open your hands.

She was afraid, despite all her words to Manukekua about how she wasn't going to hide from Kalani again. "I'm not running away from her," Liliha insisted to herself, but it was fear that made her run in the direction of Martha's house. She had money now. The sooner she got the letter to her mother, the sooner she could escape this place entirely and leave Kalani behind. She wished she could leave right that instant.

Liliha knocked on the door of Martha's house twice before it inched open. Frowning, Martha peered out with chilly eyes.

Liliha remembered how she'd spoken to Hana the last time she saw her a month ago, how angry her words were. Hana might not even *want* to see her again. Liliha's hands fidgeted against her skirt and she clasped them together to still them. "Is Hana here?"

"She's with Ahia."

"Is he still sick?"

"Yes."

She wished she had the nerve to ask Martha to write a letter, but the woman's dour face and curt words were too formidable. Liliha glanced uncertainly at the wedge of room visible behind the woman. "Would she have time—?"

"I doubt it. Ahia is very sick." Martha stared hard at her, then relented. "All right. Come in."

Liliha noticed the heat first. Walking into the room was like stepping inside a fever. She winced at the mixture of odors: bitter smoke, a stink of old fish, sweat, the sharp scent of urine.

Ahia lay on a pile of mats. A jug and a cup sat on the floor beside him, along with a small pile of rolled-up cloths. He turned over, flopping his arms and legs around until the blankets fell away. Hana, crouching beside him, drew the blankets around his shoulders again. He muttered.

"Yes, I know it's hot," Hana answered. "Because you're sick. But the last thing you need is to catch a chill." She tucked the blankets around his chin. As her hands worked, she looked over her shoulder. *"Liliha?"*

Liliha stuttered forward a step.

"I'm so glad you've come." Hana smiled warmly, but anxious shadows crouched beneath her eyes. "I've missed you."

The knot in Liliha's stomach loosened. Before she could worry about what to say or do next, she found herself kneeling beside Hana. "I missed you, too."

Hana took Liliha's hands in her own, squeezed them, let them go.

"He's worse?" Liliha said.

Hana's gaze held steady on her husband's face, on his closed eyes and the thin breath that rasped in and out between his dry lips. She rocked back on her heels and whispered, "I don't think he's going to get better, Liliha. I don't think he's going to sweat out the fever. Not even if we keep him close and warm and give him the best food we have. I've seen it before." She pressed her hand against Ahia's forehead. "It's too hot to think in here," she said, rising. She led Liliha past Martha, who sat in a chair, her head bent over a bundle of sewing.

Outside, Hana leaned against the house. Her skin was slick. "I feel like a steamed fish," she said. "I don't like to keep the room so hot except that I keep praying somehow he'll sweat the sickness out." She pulled at the front of her dress where it stuck to her skin.

Liliha flushed. "I'm sorry," she said. "About the last time I was here."

"Oh," Hana said, waving one hand dismissively. "It wasn't worth your worry."

Liliha was even more embarrassed. She'd thought Hana might be mad at her. And all that time, with Ahia getting sicker and sicker, Hana would have only been thinking about him.

Then Liliha remembered. "Oh." She fumbled with the clasp at the back of her neck. "This is for you. I was wearing it so I wouldn't lose it."

Hana bowed her head and Liliha fastened the necklace on her. Hana touched the cross; it looked tiny next to her thick fingers. "Where did you find such a beautiful thing?" Hana asked.

"I traded for it."

"Thank you. This will help me, I know."

Liliha nodded. "Are you going back to the hospital?"

"I don't know. Not while Ahia is so ill. After . . . maybe." Her face darkened. "I just have to wait."

Liliha shifted from one foot to the other, not sure what to say.

Hana's hand was warm on her arm. "How have you been, Liliha? Here I am, going on about myself and you haven't told me how you are. Do you still fish?"

"Sometimes."

"And you're living in your hut."

"Yes."

"And you managed to acquire a very fine pair of shoes. Did you trade for those, too?"

Liliha nodded. "But my mother's shawl is gone."

"Her shawl?"

"It was pink."

Hana closed her eyes, nodding. "Yes, I remember it. It looked lovely on you. So elegant."

"Kalani stole it."

Hana's eyebrows knit together. "Are you sure it was Kalani?"

"Yes!"

"I see." Hana sagged against the wall. "That poor creature."

"Who?"

"Kalani."

"Poor?" Liliha didn't understand.

"It must be horrible for her. So filled with hate and anger. Consumed by it."

Now Liliha sank against the wall beside Hana. She couldn't feel sorry for someone as vicious as Kalani. "But she took my shawl. My *mother's* shawl."

Hana fingered the cross cradled in the hollow of her throat. "But she didn't take your mother's love. Or your love for your mother."

"You think what she did was right?"

Hana turned to face Liliha. She enclosed the girl's hands within her own. "No. What she did was wrong. But is it something to fight for? Worth letting yourself be dragged into the same anger? How is that going to help you, Liliha?"

Liliha was silent.

"Don't let her have that kind of power over you." Hana squeezed Liliha's hands hard and released them. "If that doesn't convince you—well, think about it in practical terms. Choose your battles wisely. Some might be worth fighting, but plenty aren't."

Liliha rubbed her forehead. It was starting to ache. The sunlight blazing off the water pierced her eyes.

"Liliha."

"Yes?"

"You're very quiet. Is there something else?" Hana regarded her with warm, observant eyes.

Liliha gathered her courage. Hana was her friend. There was no reason to be afraid to ask her this question. Except, of course, that if she said no, Liliha didn't know where she could turn next.

"I—I wanted to ask you something, a favor, but you have so much to—so much to do right now that I—"

"What favor?"

"Hana, I need for you to write a letter for me. And keep it a secret."

"Liliha?"

"I'm asking you because I know I can trust you." *And I'm afraid to ask Martha,* Liliha added silently.

"My handwriting isn't the most beautiful. Ahia is the one with the writing. Like a work of art," Hana reflected. "Do you want the letter today?"

Liliha thought about Ahia sweating on the pillow inside the house. Even now Liliha could tell from the way Hana leaned forward that she was anxious to go back inside to her husband. Disappointment crept through Liliha. She was tired of being patient, tired of waiting. But she said, "It doesn't have to be today."

Hana swayed toward the door and shook her head. "I'm sure Martha will be glad to help."

Liliha didn't know whether to be nervous or jubilant. She didn't want anything to do with Martha, but it might be better if Hana knew nothing of her plans.

"She's the one with the paper and ink anyway," Hana continued. "And you can trust her. If she gives her word on anything, she won't break it. If you ask her to keep a secret, she will." Hana held up a hand to stop Liliha from following.

"Maybe it would be better if the two of you went somewhere, where no one else will be around to overhear."

Hana disappeared inside. Liliha tried to think the letter through, but it was hard. She didn't really know what letters were supposed to be like. How could she describe things so her mother would understand? And what would Martha think?

When the door opened again, Martha stepped outside, carrying a pen, ink, and a narrow sheet of paper with ragged edges. Her face looked grimmer than ever. She said, "We can go inside the church. No one will hear."

The church wasn't much larger than the houses, although it did boast a taller door with a window at either side and, nailed above the entrance, a cross made of red *koa* wood. Martha headed down the narrow aisle; a pair of rough benches crowded against it. She kneeled by one bench as if it were a table, arranged the paper on it, and opened the ink bottle. Then she gestured for Liliha to sit.

Liliha started to jig one foot against the floor. What should she say?

Martha lifted the pen. "You don't have to worry about my discretion," she said. "I give you my word."

Liliha watched the dust motes floating in the light. "How did you learn to write?" she asked.

"My parents worked with a mission topside, over the *pali,* in a village on the south side of the island. The missionaries taught all of us English and how to read and write. If you can't read, then how are you to read God's Word?"

"Did you ever have a Hawaiian name?"

"Only when I was very little. My parents changed it to Martha. They hoped I would grow up to be a useful person."

Liliha pondered that, but couldn't figure out what the name had to do with usefulness. "What *was* your name?"

Martha gave a short, humorless laugh and tapped the pen against the ink bottle. "I don't remember."

"So why do you live here?"

"I used to come over with the minister when he preached. He finally decided I should stay and keep the Word strong. The Christian *kama'āina* who lived here needed someone from the mission to stay."

"Do you ever want to leave?"

"No." Martha waited, looking at Liliha, then at the paper. "We should start the letter, don't you think?"

Liliha wondered what usefulness she was keeping Martha from at that very moment and fixed her gaze on her own hands. "Mother," she began. Then stopped.

The pen scratched the single word on the paper. Martha glanced up, then down at the paper again, pen poised, waiting.

Liliha closed her eyes hard to make herself see her mother. *She's sitting right there in front of you,* she told herself. *Not Martha.*

She drew a deep breath. "I've wanted to talk to you so much ever since I came to Kalaupapa. Now that I am, I don't know what to tell you about this place except that I shouldn't be here. I want to come home. Well, at least be *close* to home. I've learned to do things for myself here. I could live by myself if I had to. Uncle Malietoa would never have to know. No one would have to know but you."

"Slower," Martha said, pen flying across the paper.

Liliha paused. If she told her mother about the terrible things she'd seen in this place, her mother would worry herself to death. But if Liliha *didn't* tell her, how would her mother ever understand how serious Liliha was about wanting—needing—to come home?

"There are people here who are *so* sick and the hospital doesn't have any doctors, hardly any medicine. I saw a man who had sores on his legs, like the skin had been cut open, and there were worms crawling in them. And the *faces* on some of the people. It's worse than Grandmother ever was. I don't know how to make you see them. You wouldn't want to see them."

"Slower," Martha said.

"I've heard that sometimes people come from outside. Visitors. They come to Kalaupapa over the *pali* or by boat and stay in secret, just for a little while. I think I could find a way for us to do this. I have some money and I've built a hut of my own. I want you to come."

Liliha was shaking. Sweat dripped down her face, fell from her chin onto her hands, which were clenched against her thighs. She peered at Martha, who continued to write, face impassive. Should she tell about Kalani? About the Captain? But how could she make her mother *see*? There was no time and what she'd already put into the letter would be so hard for her mother to hear. Guilt seeped through Liliha's thoughts. Her mother must already be grieving. What would this do to her?

"I *am* all right, though. I'm hungry sometimes"—*all the time,* she mentally inserted—"but not starving. I just—I just want to come home with you. That's all."

Liliha waited until Martha's pen came to rest. "Is that all I need?" she asked.

"The usual practice would be to finish with 'Love, Liliha,' or 'Respectfully yours,' or something similar."

"All right."

"Can you sign your name? No? Then I'll write it for you."

Martha set the paper to one side to dry while she sealed the jar of ink. Liliha edged nearer to the paper. She looked at the black lines that curved and cut across it. It was hard to think that those lines were the words she'd just spoken.

"You can go ahead and pick it up," Martha instructed. "Just hold it by the edge and don't touch the ink until it's dry."

Liliha held the paper gingerly between thumb and forefinger, handling it with the same sort of reverence that Hana had for the cross on the necklace. The ink glistened.

"I need to get back to my work," Martha said.

Inside the house, Hana was sitting on the floor beside Ahia. His eyes were bright. "What about *poi*?" Hana asked him. "Would you like that?"

Liliha stepped quietly to the middle of the room. She faced Hana's back, but said nothing to interfere. Martha immediately took up her sewing.

"I'll make the *poi* then," Hana said, turning toward the fire. The light caught her face in a grimace of sorrow that shocked Liliha.

Hana busied herself with the *poi*. "Are you hungry, Liliha?" Uncomfortable, Liliha shook her head.

Hana filled a bowl and carried it to Ahia. She leaned back beside him, lifting his head in the crook of her arm so that he would be able to swallow without choking, and fed him tiny portions from her fingertips. Ahia hardly chewed at all, just pushed his lower jaw back and forth a couple of times. When he'd finished, Hana set the bowl to one side and lowered his head back onto the pillow.

Liliha, uneasy that she was witnessing something too intimate, waited on the other side of the room.

Hana stroked Ahia's closed eyelids until he fell asleep. Then she picked up the empty bowl, set it with some other dirty dishes, and approached Liliha. "Did you get the letter?" Liliha rustled the piece of paper. "Good." Hana dropped onto a chair. "You know, Liliha, the reason I'm not asking who the letter is for is because I don't want to pry."

"You wouldn't be prying." Liliha held the paper carefully on her lap like a toddler that might run off at any moment and stumble into a fire or drown in the sea. "It's for my mother."

"Can she read?"

"No. But there's a mission in the next village. Somebody there will help her."

"Yes, I'm sure somebody will." Hana leaned forward, her forearms resting against the tabletop, her hands loosely clasped. Her fingers still glistened stickily where Ahia had eaten from them. "How are you going to send it to her?"

"I was hoping that when the next ship comes, one of the sailors might take it back to Honolulu."

"And then?"

"There must be a Presbyterian church in Honolulu," Liliha said. She pronounced the long, foreign word carefully. "I think they could get it to the mission, the one that's closest to my village. The missionaries are Presbyterian. And someone from the mission could read it to my mother." Now that she'd spoken the plan aloud, it seemed almost impossible, the letter passing through too many pairs of hands.

"I'm sure your mother would be happy to hear from you."

"Yes," Liliha said after only the smallest hesitation.

"Liliha." Hana's voice was serious. "You aren't going to try to go back there, are you?"

Liliha was suddenly thankful that Martha had been the one to take down the letter. She couldn't tell Hana the truth now. Hana might want to take the letter away from her.

"No. I won't go back home." Well, that wasn't a complete falsehood, anyway. She wouldn't go back to Uncle Malietoa's.

Hana caught her in a scrutinizing gaze, then finally nodded and relaxed. "I wish you could think of this as home. Things would be easier for you then."

Liliha wanted to protest that the hardest thing in the world would be to call Kalaupapa home, to give up all hope of escape. She stayed silent. Hana had enough troubles.

"I don't know when I'll be at the hospital again," Hana said. "But you can visit me here." She fingered the cross. "And thank you for this."

Outside, the air was fresh and cool and Liliha breathed it greedily. As she walked to her hut, she held the paper in front of her face, reassuring herself that the words written on it hadn't disappeared.

Chapter Eighteen

Winter came during the next two months, and with it came storms.

Winds from the south and the west snatched grass from Liliha's roof, which she hurried to replace before rain turned the inside of her hut to mud. Wind tore at the sea, roughening the surf so that ships rarely came. When a ship *did* appear, the crew tossed casks of supplies overboard to float ashore. No rowboats. No sailors. And so Liliha's letter stayed where she'd hidden it, in a deep crevice that she'd hacked into a tree trunk and patched over with moss.

True to her vow not to run away from Kalani, she ventured away from her hut. She always watched for Kalani, but never saw her. The man who had guarded the hut greeted the rations now, not Kalani. Rumors passed around that Kalani was sick, that she had the fever, that she'd died and Opuhumanuu had hidden the body. Others claimed that she'd escaped or that she was holed up in her hut, cleaning a store of guns and sharpening knives.

Liliha was just happy not to see her.

She was still nervous all the time, though. When she was in her own hut, she thought about how Kalani knew where she lived and could show up at any time in a fury. Whenever Liliha left the hut, she wondered if this would be the day that her path would cross Kalani's.

She used her new net, tearing it twice on rocks hidden beneath the churning water, rips she did her best to mend. She caught little and, many days, wasn't able to venture far enough out into the water to catch anything at all. The new net was a help when the weather was good, but during the stormy season she might as well have used Pauahi's old one.

She was hungry, but then just about everyone was. When Liliha set out her carvings in the compound, no one wanted to trade away a single grain of rice or a sliver of dried beef. Manukekua sneaked small packages of beef and salmon out of the Captain's house to Liliha whenever he could. For the first couple of weeks after returning down the *pali,* they had been stiff and silent with each other. Manukekua would ask her to take the food with a simple "please" and Liliha would accept with a quiet "thank you" and a nod.

Gradually, they began to speak more. They never talked about Liliha's mother or escape, but concentrated instead on the scant food supplies, the starved corpses carried from the hospital each day.

"The Captain's making people bury them," Manukekua said to her one day during the worst stretch of the stormy season. He pointed at the graveyard just past the fence. Liliha shivered. With its shallow, churned-up dirt, its absence of greenery or markers, the graveyard was a bleak spot even on the sunniest day. There were few mourners, and the gravediggers— lepers and *kōkuas* alike—were sullen and slow, pressed into service and none too eager to work hard at the unpleasant chore.

"There are a lot of bodies," Manukekua added. "Always worse during the storms. The winds get too cold, it's too wet . . ."

"And hardly anything to eat," Liliha lamented.

"If more supplies don't come soon, I'm going back topside."

Liliha nodded. "I saw two men on the *pali* trail yesterday."

"Going or coming?"

"Going. I wonder what they trade?"

"I don't know." Manukekua peered between two boards of the fence. The gap was wide enough that even from where she sat Liliha could see the dark blue of the Captain's coat as he stalked back and forth, glaring at the gravediggers.

"I'll bring food for you, I promise," Manukekua said, backing away from the fence. "And I can take some of your carvings for trade. If I go."

Liliha looked down at her feet and then away again. Her shoes were scuffed, the soles clumped with mud, and one of the buttons had already twisted loose and dangled by a thread. The skin at the back of her ankles had toughened up and the blisters had healed. Although the shoes protected her feet from cuts and splinters, they couldn't stop the numbness from deepening. Liliha stumbled more often when she walked now. She wondered how well she'd handle the long walk to the southern side of the island.

She bit off a hunk of beef and chewed. Manukekua watched her with concern. "You said you got your rations last time, didn't you?"

She swallowed. "I don't know what would have happened if

Kalani had been there, but it was just Opuhumanuu." She could still feel the relief that had rushed through her that day at the shore when she'd realized Kalani wasn't anywhere in sight. Opuhumanuu wasn't frightening, scurrying in to fetch a few rations and then darting away.

"I heard she was sick," Manukekua said. "But I saw her at the graveyard yesterday." Liliha froze. She'd hoped Kalani's absence would go on forever. "She was taking clothes from one of the bodies before they buried him." His eyes met Liliha's. "So if she *was* sick—and I think she was—she must be getting better now. She looked pretty bad, though. Her head seemed like it was all shrunken and skinny. The skin like this"—he pulled his own skin tight so the bones jutted against it. "But she was yelling, just like always."

Liliha's appetite vanished. She rewrapped the beef Manukekua had given her and stashed it in her sack. Better to save the food. She'd had good luck getting her rations that month when the supplies were simply floated ashore. She'd had to push and shove, even claw, but there had been no Kalani wielding a club, and the other bullies had been busy with other victims.

If Kalani came to the landing site next time, there was no telling what would happen to Liliha's share of food. She could ask Manukekua to get rations for her, but she had to be there in case a sailor came ashore.

Blue flashed and the Captain stomped around the end of the fence. Mud covered his boots and spattered his pants. Manukekua squeezed Liliha's arm and slipped back into the house. Liliha sprang up and to one side just as the Captain passed without even glancing at her.

She might as well sit and carve on the shore at Kalaupapa landing and hope for rations to arrive. The supply ship was a good week overdue as it was.

On her way, she stopped to pull the letter from its hiding place and, checking the money deep in her skirt pocket, limped to Kalaupapa. She settled onto a rise at the top of the beach and began to carve. Along the shore in both directions, lepers crouched, waiting, their faces straight to the sea. People were hungry and determined to have first grab at any supplies.

The first shout was like an *i'iwi's* cry, a high squeak. The second was jubilant. Liliha's hand rose to her throat. A ship sat far out from shore. The day was cool and gray, but the ocean was calm. When a pair of rowboats nudged out from the ship and jounced across the water, Liliha leaped up. Sailors were coming ashore! After so many weeks of waiting, she might have a chance to send her letter.

Pulling the paper out from her pocket, she ran her fingers along the folds, making each crease precise. She could now see the sunburned face and blond beard of the sailor in the first boat. Why couldn't the boats come faster, before anyone else arrived at the beach, before—?

Kalani came hitching up from the road, Opuhumanuu and a tattered line of beggars lagging behind her. When the first boat drove onto the shore and the sailor began to swing crates over the side, Kalani was there. The letter seemed to turn to fire in Liliha's hand. Did she dare go so close to Kalani? What were the chances the sailor with the blond beard would speak Hawaiian anyway?

Before Liliha could take a step toward the sailor, Kalani turned and stared at her as if she'd sensed Liliha's fear. She looked like she'd passed through an illness. As Manukekua had said, Kalani's head was skeletal, her skin drawn and even more discolored, her lips permanently shrunken back from the gums. But her eyes still burned; they'd lost none of their cruelty.

"If you came for rations," Kalani shouted at Liliha, "you're not going to get them here." Kalani reached into a crate and pulled out blocks of *pa'i 'ai* and shriveled rectangles of beef. Ravenous people shoved forward, grabbing at whatever Kalani doled out to them. Some were so hungry that they tore their packages open and began to rip at the food with their nails and teeth.

Is this how it was always going to be? Kalani tormenting those sicker than herself and the sick just taking it?

Liliha shouted back, "You'd just cheat me anyway."

When she saw Kalani's face twist with fury, a strange, fearful pleasure coiled through Liliha's veins. Liliha turned to the second boat. With joy, she saw that the sailor manning it had a blunt, dark body and thick, black hair. He looked Hawaiian, and that meant they would speak the same language. A light drizzle began to fall, dimpling the ocean. Liliha slipped the paper back into her pocket to protect it and waded into the ankle-deep water. She had a chance.

Waves splashed over the tops of her shoes, drenched her skirt below the knees. Her thoughts were perfectly focused: *Get to the sailor first. Talk to him. Give him the letter. Run.*

Liliha ran. The rough shore and her own numb feet nearly pitched her off balance as she spurted forward.

When she reached the boat, the sailor was swinging his legs over the side. Liliha forgot to speak, just yanked the letter from her pocket and mutely extended it to him.

Eyeing her, the sailor pulled a tin from his pocket and wadded a plug of tobacco into his cheek. "What is it?" he said, laughing. "A love note?" He plucked the paper neatly from her grasp. She felt suddenly stripped.

Her cheeks burned and she frantically shook her head even as she realized, with relief, that she understood his words and that he didn't seem alarmed at touching something a leper had held.

"Too bad," he said. "I never mind getting a love letter."

"It's for my mother," she burst out. "Would you take it to her? Here"—she fumbled in the skirt pocket—"I can pay." She opened her fingers to show the money that lay on her palm.

The sailor regarded the money. He shifted the tobacco wad to the other side of his mouth. His cheek bulged with sudden malignancy. "Well, now that depends on where your mother is."

"You'd just have to go to Honolulu."

"That's where I'm headed anyway." He reached for the money.

"To the Presbyterian church," she added. His hand wavered. "Give the letter to the people there and ask them if they can get it to the mission at Waianae. Someone at the mission can get it to my mother. Say it's from Liliha at Kalaupapa."

"I'll have to ask around to find where any church is," the sailor said, considering. "But I can do that." He neatly emptied her hand of all the money. He tucked the letter inside his damp shirt and stuck the cash in the pocket with the tobacco tin. "You got her name here on the letter? Or your name?"

Before Liliha could answer, hoarse shouts erupted behind her and, turning, she saw Opuhumanuu laboring toward them. Others shambled behind her, eager to get at the rations. Opuhumanuu's feet sank at each step; she toiled forward and stopped in front of the sailor.

"Kalani has business with you," she told him importantly.

"Who?" the sailor asked. Opuhumanuu pointed. "Oh, her. Yes, I've seen *her* before." The sailor's mouth twitched and he released a perfect stream of juice. "Well, why doesn't she come talk to me then?"

"She's busy," Opuhumanuu answered. "With the supplies. Helping people."

The sailor peered through the misty air at Kalani, who was barking something at an old woman cowering before her. "I bet they really appreciate the help, too," the sailor said, grinning.

Opuhumanuu squared her shoulders. "She sent *me* to talk to you."

"About what?"

Opuhumanuu's eyes flicked once toward Liliha. "Certain things."

The other lepers descended on the boat; in moments all the crates were lodged in the sand or half submerged in the surf. The sailor dumped their contents, heaved the empty crates into the boat, and began to push it into the water again.

Opuhumanuu coughed. "Certain *money* things."

The sailor swung toward her. "Such as?"

She scuttled backward, sloshing through the water. When the sailor stepped after her, she leaned toward him and he bent down to listen. Liliha watched, rubbing one hand hard with the other one. She was certain she saw Opuhumanuu slide something into his hand. The sailor crouched to wash something in the water, and when he stood, he held that something up near his face. It was a large coin. Opuhumanuu nodded, her mouth split in a grotesque grin, and limped away.

"Well, good luck to you," the sailor said to Liliha. She wanted to ask him about Opuhumanuu's money, but she couldn't say a word. He pushed the boat out into the water and swung himself inside. Liliha stared after the receding shape. The sailor seemed to be shifting around on the bench, the oars dangling thin and useless as a pair of broken wings on a mosquito. Then he leaned over the side of the boat.

He held something pale in one hand. Her letter. He held the paper away from the boat. Then—Liliha couldn't be sure at such a distance, especially as the rain intensified—she thought she saw the letter fall away from his hand and disappear into the churning water.

She ran forward and didn't even notice the cold waves breaking against her until she was waist deep. She shouted, but the wind pushed her voice back at her. The sailor took up the oars and began rowing hard. He never looked back.

She stared after him, the boat shrinking into the distance until it reached the ship. Then she turned and slogged back to shore, her sodden skirt dragging.

Every step Liliha took was measured. Opuhumanuu, at the

edge of the crowd surrounding Kalani, stared nervously, her little hands drawn up to her chest. She glanced at Kalani, checking to make sure she was still nearby.

"I know what you did," Liliha told Opuhumanuu, amazed at how steady her voice stayed. Steady and cold. "I know what you paid him to do."

Opuhumanuu raised her meager eyebrows and shuffled closer to Kalani. "Who?" Opuhumanuu asked. Liliha said nothing. "Oh, that sailor?"

Liliha stepped forward, flung her arm out, and slapped Opuhumanuu hard across one cheek. Opuhumanuu stumbled backward in surprise. One crabbed hand grappled at her cheek, which turned a dark crimson. She looked up with wet, stunned eyes. When Liliha took another deliberate step forward, Opuhumanuu turned and fled to Kalani's side.

Liliha's eyes were slits. She imagined how they looked, fierce and thin as the edge of a blade. She fixed Opuhumanuu with that stare like it was the point of a spear.

"So, tell me," Liliha said, voice calm, "did Kalani order you to do that?" Opuhumanuu's chin quavered to her chest. "Or did you think of it all by yourself?" Liliha looked past her to Kalani.

Kalani jabbed at Opuhumanuu with one stringy arm. "Opu doesn't think. Do you, Opu?" Opuhumanuu shook her head miserably from side to side. Kalani laughed. "But it was a good joke, wasn't it, Opu?" She poked again at Opuhumanuu's ribs, and Opuhumanuu's head shot up; her smile was a grimace.

"You stole my mother's shawl," Liliha declared.

Kalani's eyes glinted. "Your mother's?"

Liliha's stomach cramped with hatred. Of course Kalani

couldn't have known the shawl was her mother's. The idea of it—the once frothy lace settled over Kalani's pocked skin—tore at Liliha's thoughts.

"Anyway," Kalani said, half turning away, feigning a yawn, "I'm not sure I have a shawl in my wardrobe." She glanced back at Liliha. "Not pink anyway."

Liliha's hand slid into her pocket; her fingers gripped the cool handle of the knife. She drew the knife free.

Kalani still watched her, smiling. "What have *you* ever gutted, besides a fish?"

Liliha stepped toward the smirking face, but a shriveled man crept right in front of her. "Please, Miss," he pleaded with Kalani, clutching at her sleeve.

Kalani dropped back to the crates and with a ghastly smile, as gracious as her drawn lips allowed, deposited a half brick of *pa'i 'ai* in the man's trembling hands. He fell away, bubbling thanks.

A woman with clawed hands and swollen lumps along her arms pushed in next.

"You'll have to forgive me, Liliha," Kalani said, her smile grotesque. "I have work to do."

"I'll never forgive you," Liliha spat. "And there's one thing you can be sure of. I'll have my shawl back."

But Kalani's back was turned against her already. Kalani bent over the remaining rations, rummaging together a paltry selection of food for the begging woman.

Opuhumanuu stared at the churned-up sand and rock at her feet and didn't look up until Liliha said, "You, too, Opuhumanuu. I'll never forgive you either. And I won't forget."

Opuhumanuu peeked at her with eyes that were quick and anxious. Liliha nodded at Opuhumanuu, a curt stab of the chin, shoved the knife deep in her pocket again, and angled away from shore. She stopped once, leaning forward with her hands splayed against her thighs, and gasped. Rain dropped like pebbles against her. She glanced back. Kalani was driving away the last of the beggars, cursing at them, while Opuhumanuu shoved bricks of *pa'i 'ai* into a canvas sack.

Liliha realized she hadn't gathered any rations for herself. She'd thought of nothing but the sailor and the letter, and now nothing was just what she had. Shutting her eyes, she imagined the letter swirling through dark waves, the paper softening and disintegrating.

The word "Mother" tore apart, each letter spiraling and sinking separately from the others.

CHAPTER NINETEEN

"I COULD HAVE KILLED KALANI," LILIHA SAID. "WHO would even care?"

"Opuhumanuu," answered Manukekua.

Liliha snorted. "She'd just move on to the next bully."

"I don't know." Manukekua had shut the door of the Captain's house behind him, but snores still sounded through the boards. Manukekua's eyebrows knit together and Liliha realized how sparse they'd become. Hardly a hair left. It made his forehead look higher, and shiny as bone; his eyes were huge.

Liliha stomped around to the back of the house, her hands gripping a pair of heavy buckets. Her boots sank in mud. Manukekua followed her. The wind, already strong, gathered force in the narrow channel between the house and the rotting fence. The rain, at least, had already passed through during the night. Liliha's hair spun across her face. She set the buckets down and, gathering a hank of hair in one hand, pushed the hair under her collar and down her back.

Manukekua handed her a bundle of dried beef and rice. "I'm sorry it's not more," he said.

Liliha leaned forward impulsively and kissed his cheek. When she pulled back, he watched her with startled eyes.

"Thank you," she said.

"The way the supplies have been, even the Captain hasn't been eating all that well," Manukekua observed. He eyed the buckets. "Pauahi?"

Liliha nodded. "But I'm not getting all that much food out of the deal. She's hoarding most of it. Anyway, once she finds out Kalani's been seen around, she'll get rid of me again." It had been two weeks since the last supplies came, two weeks since Liliha had tried to send her letter. Her anger hadn't diminished. "When the next boat comes, I'm taking double rations." Maybe more. And if she saw that sailor again? Fury rose in her at the thought of his carefree face, the dimples worked into each cheek, his jokes about love letters.

"Liliha?" Manukekua watched her with concern.

"Nothing," she muttered, knotting the bundle of food into her skirt so her hands would be free to carry the water. "I should go. Pauahi's waiting." She hoisted the buckets and carried them around to the front of the house.

"I'll help you," Manukekua said, reaching for one of the handles.

"It's easier if I carry them both. They balance each other."

"Liliha . . ." He looked wretched. "I'm sorry about the letter."

"I know. Thanks."

"Liliha . . ."

She waited, but before he could speak, someone shouted from across the compound. Startled, he turned; Liliha set the buckets down again.

Martha strode toward them. Liliha had never seen Martha here before. Something terrible must have happened.

"Is Hana . . . ?" Liliha plucked at the crisp cuff of Martha's shirt.

"It's Ahia," Martha said. Her voice stayed steady, her eyes flat. "He's passed over."

"He's what?"

Martha's cool eyes locked onto Liliha. "Died," she said.

Liliha could only nod.

"And Liliha's friend? Hana. How is she?" Manukekua asked.

"She has solace sufficient for her grief." Martha glanced around the compound. Her face was like a perfectly folded blanket, giving no clue to her thoughts. "She sent me here to find you. He'll be buried this afternoon. There's a small cemetery near Kalaupapa. Reverend Thomas has come from topside."

"When—when did he die?"

"Day before last."

Liliha thought of that sweltering room, and of Ahia's corpse growing cool despite the fire.

"He's luckier than most," Martha said, stepping away. "Getting a burial. A *proper* one."

Liliha shivered, thinking of the bodies she'd seen carried out of the hospital. Usually, the body was loosely wrapped in the most threadbare, worn-out blanket available, the ends of the blanket tied to a long pole hoisted onto the shoulders of two or three men. The men then carried the body to a shallow grave and slung it down into the dirt without ceremony.

Manukekua's fingers closed on Liliha's wrist. His hand was warm and Liliha was grateful for it. "Do you want me to go with you?" he asked. "I didn't really know Ahia, but—"

She didn't hesitate. "Yes."

Then Manukekua took one of the buckets after all, and they went to Pauahi's hut, where Liliha took the agreed-upon ration of salmon. She left without answering a word of Pauahi's shrill complaints.

Once at her own hut, Liliha hurriedly combed her hair and wiped off her face. She tried to imagine Hana's grief. All she could picture was a vast black crater, cold and empty. What would Hana do now? Manukekua rolled down his sleeves; the cuffs flapped around his bony wrists. He buttoned his shirt to the neck, swiped his straggly hair behind his ears, and hitched his shoulders.

When they arrived at Kalaupapa landing, the inhabitants were gathered just beyond the last house. A minister in a black coat, worn shiny at the elbows, stood in front of the mourners with his back to them. Hana waited just behind him. She leaned slightly against Martha, engulfed Martha's skinny arm with her own solid one. Hana's hair was cinched back as tightly as Martha's, a few strands had wisped loose and floated around her face. Her face was as impossible for Liliha to read as a page of Martha's writing.

They'd wrapped the body in a clean canvas sheet, cream-colored and free of holes. He lay stiff on a plank hoisted onto the shoulders of four men. The minister paced forward, not looking back. Hana pulled her arm free of Martha's and hurried ahead to walk beside the body.

The procession moved steadily to a field nearby. Liliha had seen it before, but never paid much attention to it. A dozen low wooden crosses stood in two tidy rows. Someone had already dug the hole. Liliha leaned forward, peering past a man's shoulder, and saw roots bristling from the rim of the hole like stubborn beards.

"It's deep enough," Manukekua whispered. Liliha knew what he meant. Deep enough that hard rains wouldn't wash it free. Liliha drew back. It made her dizzy to look into that hole, made her stomach sour and sick to think of Ahia within it.

The pallbearers set the board onto the ground. A long piece of rope had been tied through a hole at each corner of the board, and now the men gripped those ropes to suspend it above the grave.

The minister spoke. His words were like the Captain's: English. His voice was low, resonant; it made Liliha think of deep salt water with mysterious creatures moving through it. Hana was squinting, her eyes wet. The pallbearers lowered the body.

Liliha tugged Manukekua back behind the other mourners. "What's he saying?" she whispered.

Manukekua chewed his lip as he thought. When he spoke, his translation came slowly. "Stay awake, for you know neither the day nor the hour."

Liliha shook her head. "What does *that* mean?"

"It means he's dead," a voice hissed from behind her, the words borne on breath so foul that Liliha almost gagged. She whipped around. Kalani's face, sharp and skeletal, pushed near to her own. Her eyes had changed, a thick mucus oozing over the lower lids, and her skin radiated a sickly heat. Kalani grinned. Her gums glistened purple as jellyfish. "And it's a warning," she added, still smiling. "You never know when you're going to die."

Liliha stumbled back. Manukekua, moving beside her, caught her arm.

"It could be in a year," Kalani mused, bending back one finger, then the others. "Or a week. Tomorrow. Tonight." She blinked at the sky. "Before the sun sets today. Who knows?"

Manukekua grabbed Liliha's arm and squeezed. Liliha broke away. In that instant, she realized that the minister had stopped talking. The faces of the pallbearers had turned toward Liliha and, past her, to Kalani.

Kalani strutted forward, Opuhumanuu just behind. Kalani reached back to grab something from Opuhumanuu's hands. She shook open a flurry of pink that gradually settled across her knobby shoulders.

Liliha's face prickled, numbed. *My shawl.*

Kalani gripped the lacy border and drew the shawl tighter. A brown stain smeared the length of the garment; snapped threads waved in the breeze like seaweed in a tide. Kalani preened, stretching her neck to one side, then the other. She stepped to the very edge of the grave and stared at the body. The minister coughed and swayed forward, speaking to Kalani, who silenced him with a single, slit-eyed glance.

"My condolences," she rasped to Hana, who waited, motionless, on the other side of the grave. Hana's eyes burned with pain, but she held her mouth steady, her expression composed. Kalani gave her a shrewd look. "But you knew he'd be food for worms soon enough, didn't you? I could tell it as soon as you came ashore."

When the minister grabbed for Kalani's arm, she stepped neatly away from him. His cheeks were red, his jaw clenched.

The mourners murmured, peering at Kalani with shocked faces. Hana had flinched at the phrase "food for worms," but she was now steady again, regarding Kalani with clear eyes.

"Is that all you cared for him, pitching him down a hole in that old sheet?" Kalani said to her.

"Evil." The minister found his tongue at last. He spoke Hawaiian now, and Liliha wondered why he'd bothered with English before. Did he look down on Hawaiians the way the Captain did? "You are an evil creature."

Kalani laughed and held up the mutilated shawl. "Here. Give him something soft to sleep on in the dark." With a sudden, swift movement, she dropped the shawl into the grave.

"That's mine!" Liliha shrieked. She ran full force into Kalani, nearly knocking her down. Liliha's fists drove like pistons. Tears smeared her vision; hair tangled in her lashes, blinding her. Blood roared through her head. Something smashed into her gut, locking her breath in her lungs, but still her fists drove forward.

"Liliha!" Hana's voice broke through the welter of Liliha's own blood, and Liliha's arms were suddenly pinned behind her. Hana had one, Manukekua the other. A pair of men held Kalani back. Between Kalani and Liliha, the minister fumed. He paced one way, then the other, rumbling foreign words.

Liliha turned toward the grave, wrested herself free, and kneeled at the edge. The white parcel of Ahia's corpse lay at the bottom, rolled to one side of the pit. Grimy pink lace and yarn partially covered him.

"Liliha." Hana pulled her back. "It's done. Leave it."

Liliha turned furious eyes on Kalani. Kalani's mouth was open, the tip of her tongue working at a loose front tooth.

"She stole it," Liliha choked. "She stole everything."

Hana's palm stroked her hair. "Let it go, Liliha. That's past."

"It will never be past."

Martha came from the head of the grave, shaking her head. "I've never seen anything like it," she said, not deigning to look at Liliha or Kalani. "The disrespect for the dead." Kneeling, she scooped up a handful of dirt and opened her fingers over the grave. Dirt thudded against the canvas sheet like a sudden, hard cloudburst. The minister stepped beside her, raised his hands, closed his eyes, and began talking.

Manukekua bent near to Liliha, whispered in a soothing voice, "He's praying now. Do you want to know what he's saying?"

Liliha shook her head. If she spoke, she'd start crying again and she refused to give Kalani the satisfaction. Kalani's tongue finally fished her front tooth completely loose. She spat the tooth in Liliha's direction.

"You'll pay for that," Kalani said. Her face was rigid, her body shaking. "And it won't come cheap." She wrenched her arms free, whirled around, and stalked away, Opuhumanuu slinking after her.

"Liliha," Hana said gently, clucking her tongue and stroking the girl's hair.

Martha made a clucking sound as well, but it was harsh. "Isn't it enough that she's burying her husband today," she said, pushing her face close to Liliha's, "without you disrupting the funeral?"

Liliha flushed. "But it was Kalani."

Martha flung up her hands and turned to follow the minister, who, having concluded his prayer, stomped back toward the settlement. One of the pallbearers picked up a shovel and began to toss dirt into the hole.

"Hana?"

"It's all right, Liliha."

"I didn't mean to—I'm sorry I ruined—"

"Hush. I know she stole that shawl from you."

Manukekua crouched to pick up Kalani's broken tooth. Holding it lightly between thumb and forefinger, he squinted at the jagged, yellow bit of bone smeared pink with blood.

"She'll come after you," he told Liliha.

"I know." Liliha was amazed at how calm she sounded. Her head pounded and something close to panic buzzed up and down her arms and legs, making her long to run and run.

"You have to stay with us tonight," Hana said decisively.

"No."

"Liliha, child, listen to reason."

Liliha turned her head to look at the grave. The last corner of lace disappeared under a hail of dirt.

"I have my own hut," she said, facing Hana and Manukekua. Manukekua's scant eyebrows rose in alarm and he tossed the broken tooth into the weeds.

Hana tried again. "Liliha, you have to—"

"I don't have to do *anything*," she answered. Mute eyes watched her. She felt giddy and frightened at the same time, veering out of control.

"But for one night. If you would just—" Hana started. Liliha cut her off with the wave of a hand. She could imagine Martha's sour face. Liliha didn't want to be around her, didn't want to sleep in the suffocating room where Ahia died.

"She could kill you this time," Manukekua protested.

Liliha was afraid, but anger like fire burned deep inside her. She stared at Manukekua and Hana. "What if I kill her first?"

They stared back, not even blinking until Hana broke the silence with a single, stunned word. "Jesus."

Liliha pushed herself into motion, ignoring the path, plowing off into the weeds.

Manukekua burst after her, babbling. "Liliha, you can't—what are you talking about? She's—Liliha! Wait!"

"Liliha." Hana's measured voice stopped her. Liliha turned. Hana's face was somber, no longer shocked. Behind her, some of the other mourners had begun trailing home; others waited for Hana.

"Don't do it," Hana said. "Promise me."

"She started it."

"You can't be serious, Liliha. You can't be talking of murder. You're twelve years old!"

"Thirteen now." At least, she *thought* she must have turned thirteen by now.

"It's against the law," Hana protested.

Liliha clenched her eyes shut. Against her eyelids, she could see that first early morning on shore, the bobbing lanterns, could smell the reek of rotting flesh, could hear the shrill voices tearing into the perpetual wind and a single rasping voice speaking to her.

She opened her eyes. "In this place there *is* no law."

Hana's face twisted. "God's law, Liliha, God's law."

"I don't understand that."

"Of course you do."

"She made fun of Ahia. She made fun of him while he was being buried. How can you just pretend that didn't happen?"

"I know what happened," Hana said.

"But you ignore it."

Hana shook her head, a single, graceful movement. Her face was composed again. "No. I forgive it."

"But—"

"And I don't let it possess me."

"I hate her." Just saying the three flat words sent an exhilarating surge of fury and power through Liliha's body.

"That's *your* misfortune, not hers."

With a wordless cry, Liliha spun away.

"Liliha!" Hana called after her. "Liliha, I'm sorry!"

Liliha strode inland toward the *pali*. Her feet were numb and clumsy and several times she staggered over tufts of grass and weed. Tears burned along her cheeks, but she didn't know why she was crying. How did she feel? She couldn't unravel the emotions tangling inside her heart: hatred, rage, grief, fear.

Footsteps padded just behind her and she reared around, eyes frantic.

"I'll stay with you tonight," Manukekua said, raising his hands to calm her though his own eyes were wide and white. "I'll stay."

Liliha nodded, walked even faster. Manukekua matched her stride. She swallowed hard, a lump stuck halfway down her throat.

I'm sorry.

She saw a heavy face, the eyes curved gently downward at each corner, eyes that wouldn't meet Liliha's. Her mother's face. Her mother leaving her at Kalihi Hospital, leaving her with the words "I'm sorry," and the creak and rattle of the cart pulling away. The wheeze of the horse's breath.

Her eyes burned.

She saw her mother's eyes, black and full as wet stones. Black eyes watching Liliha bend beneath Uncle Malietoa's insults. Watching Liliha take a final, angry step into the hut where Grandmother waited, the old woman's leprous fingers upraised, pincerlike, ready to torment Liliha, orders already snapping from the old woman's mouth.

Why hadn't her mother ever *said* anything? Why hadn't she stopped Malietoa?

When she reached her house, Liliha collapsed on the damp floor, unfastened her shoes, and yanked them off. She grabbed the bottle of medicine, upended it, shook it ferociously until the rest of the ointment oozed out, then tossed the bottle against the grass wall. She rubbed the medicine into her feet and legs until they glistened with oil in the dim room.

Then she rocked back and forth, her face tight with anguish. Both feet were numb. Entirely numb. *The feet of a corpse,* Liliha thought as she rocked herself.

In the darkness, Manukekua's hand cupped her chin. His mouth was soft and light against her lips. "I'll check outside," he said, stepping away, his body a dark sliver sliding through the doorway.

Tears shook from Liliha's eyes until her cheeks were soaked. She heard Manukekua's feet trampling on weeds and, after what seemed like a long time, a quiet beginning rain whispering in the leaves.

CHAPTER TWENTY

THE HOUSE SHOOK.

Liliha jerked awake. "Manukekua?" she said blankly, peering into the darkness where an even darker shape hulked.

Fear slit Liliha's stomach. She tried to stand up, gasping at the pain in her bruised belly. Something smashed into the wall beside her. Bits of grass puffed into the air, the dust moist and sour.

A scream locked in Liliha's throat. She rolled to one side; something stopped her movement. Groping blindly with one hand, she touched fine hair, sticky and wet at the scalp.

"Manukekua?" she gasped.

"Not much of a guard." Liliha knew the mocking laugh. A club smashed down, striking at Liliha's left forearm. Liliha cried out at the shock of pain.

"Did you think I'd let you get away with it?" Kalani's words sounded odd, lisping, and Liliha remembered the missing front tooth. "Do you really think you're as strong as I am? Just waiting for me to get sick enough so you can kill me and steal my things?"

Kalani raised the club again. Liliha twisted away just as it slammed down. The club stuck in the wall. As Kalani jerked it free, Liliha scrambled to her feet. She paused at the door, a cool wind swiping sweat from her face. The clouds were gone. Liliha's eyes, adjusting to the pale starlight, made out Manukekua's body slumped against the wall across from the door. His head lolled onto one shoulder. She couldn't see his face.

"Manukekua?"

She took a single, quivering step toward him when Kalani rushed at her.

Liliha barreled out of her hut toward the dark face of the *pali*. She heard Kalani cursing behind her. As Liliha ran, she moved the fingers of her left hand. The fingers seemed all right, but she didn't know about her arm. Pain pulsed through it from elbow to wrist. She glanced back. Kalani was no more than twenty paces behind. Opuhumanuu scuttled in Kalani's wake.

Liliha reached the muddy trail, dashed up it. Her feet nearly skidded out from under her as she dared another look back. Kalani was gaining, advancing as relentlessly as a long-legged insect.

Liliha glanced wildly around. Ahead was the trail, gradually climbing. To the right of the path, the cliff rose nearly vertical; to the left, the *pali* plunged downward into darkness. Trying to leave the trail and climb sideways across the *pali* face would be treacherous, but if she kept to the path, Kalani would overtake her—and soon.

Liliha left the path. She moved slowly, gripping at vines and roots with both hands despite the pain in her left arm. If she lost a handhold, if her feet slipped, she would plunge to the bottom of the cliff.

Kalani didn't hesitate. She drove her feet into the knotty vegetation and clambered after Liliha. Even Opuhumanuu moved with surprising speed as she overtook Kalani.

Liliha's face pressed against the *pali*. She smelled dirt and darkness.

She had to *move*.

But when she tried, her exhausted legs spasmed, pulling her feet loose, and she grappled hard at a nest of vines just above her head, managing to clutch them just in time to stop her fall. She clung to that spot, forced herself to hold her breath and listen.

She heard moisture dripping onto leaves and the far-off rush of a waterfall. Then came Opuhumanuu's voice, shockingly close.

"You won't take her place. You won't live long enough."

A hand snatched at her. Without thought, Liliha let go. Vines slithered through her fingers and she was sliding down the *pali*. Protruding rocks bruised her ribs and cracked against her knees.

And then, so abruptly that she didn't know what had happened, she stopped.

Staggering to her feet, Liliha peered at the ledge on which she'd landed. Behind her, the ledge dropped off into vast, empty space. Her left arm hurt worse than ever.

Liliha heard vines snap, leaves rattle, then Opuhumanuu

was on the ledge. She stared across at Liliha, who fumbled at her skirt and pulled the knife free. Liliha gripped it in her right fist, the blade upright as a stalk of cane, the tip even with her chin.

Opuhumanuu edged closer, eyeing the knife, crouching like a wrestler. "Aren't you sorry now?" Opuhumanuu said in a childish singsong. "Aren't you sorry now?"

Liliha tried to edge backward. She knew there was only air beneath her heels. She waited at the very rim of the ledge.

With a volcano of curses, Kalani dropped onto the ledge just behind Opuhumanuu, who sidled off slightly to the left. In the moonlight, Kalani's face seemed made of bone.

"You didn't have to hurt Manukekua," Liliha said. Her voice broke.

"Hurt him?" Kalani said. "I hope he's dead."

Liliha's hand was so slick she could barely hold on to the knife.

Opuhumanuu was close to her now, not much more than an arm's length away. "Aren't you *really* sorry now?" Opuhumanuu was cagey, bobbing forward and back, staying just out of Liliha's reach.

"He's dead," Kalani said. She bent over her ribs as if they hurt, but she still managed to grip the club. "And you're dead, too."

She hurtled forward, the club rising high over her head.

The knife dropped from Liliha's hand. She didn't know if it slipped or if she let it fall. She dodged to one side, cracking into Opuhumanuu, knocking her to the ground at Kalani's feet.

Kalani stumbled over Opuhumanuu and, arms pinwheeling, the club flying off into a tree, Kalani disappeared over the edge. Branches erupted with shrill insect cries.

Liliha heard a short crack, and a scream that cut off abruptly. Ducking her head over the ledge, she saw bushes and branches shake as Kalani's body smashed through them. Then, quiet, except for the wind pushing at the trees and the first, tentative cries of an o'o.

Her face glistening with tears, Opuhumanuu crawled beside Liliha.

"What did you do?" Opuhumanuu croaked. Liliha's mouth worked helplessly. "What am I going to do?" Opuhumanuu gripped a fistful of vines and inched off the ledge, following Kalani.

Liliha picked up the knife, huddled with her knees to her chest until she stopped shaking. Her arm throbbed, but she no longer felt like fainting. When she peered from the ledge again, she saw no one at first. Then movement. A long, twisted shape in the shadows.

Kalani lay at the crooked base of a tree, caught in its roots like a stick in a hand. Opuhumanuu hovered above Kalani's smashed legs, her wrenched arm. Kalani tried to push herself up. Her head swayed drunkenly with the effort, lolled back, collapsed.

A single thought started Liliha shivering again, pushed her into motion.

Manukekua. Blood on his scalp, his hair drenched with it. He wasn't dead. He couldn't be dead.

She edged sideways away from the ledge, moving cautiously

until she'd worked her way back to the path. She ran, not caring if her dead feet caught on rocks or tripped over vines, not caring if she fell, ignoring the searing pain in her arm.

She forgot Kalani, forgot Opuhumanuu, forgot to fear them. Even forgot to hate them.

"Let him be alive." She whispered the words over and over, praying to something—she didn't know what. But praying.

Chapter Twenty-one

"She wants her hair," Hana said, nudging her head toward Kalani, who curled, shivering, on a mat just inside the hospital door.

"Her *what?*" With her good hand, Liliha scooped a ladle through the water bucket and, without looking, held the ladle to a girl's cracked lips. Liliha's left arm was wrapped in strips of old cloth holding the mending bones in position. The arm ached all the time. Still, she supposed that was better than the headaches Manukekua had suffered for the last two months. At first his headaches had been excruciating and constant; it was only in the last couple of weeks that they'd eased.

"Her hair," Hana answered, dabbing at a man's ulcerated arm with a damp rag. She pointed at another woman on a frayed mat halfway down the room. "I think she wants water, too. Liliha, could you . . . ?"

Why was it still so hard to be in this building, Liliha wondered, pushing the dipper through the water again. She'd been coming into the hospital almost every day so Hana could check her arm and inspect the bandages. The odor rising from the bodies of the sick still made Liliha gag. How did Hana breathe in the stench so easily? How did she touch the sores? Liliha watched her with wonder.

"But Kalani doesn't have any hair," Liliha pointed out. "Well, hardly any."

"She used to. She told me."

Squinting against the glare from the doorway, Liliha stared hard at Kalani. Kalani had a broken leg, a fractured arm, splintered ribs. Gashes gouged deep into her skin had succumbed to a raging infection. Fever swam through her until sweat poured from her face and her eyes rolled white. She raved and, between fits of delirium, went rigid with pain. Terror caught Liliha's heart: terror at the depth of Kalani's suffering and terror that she would miraculously recover.

"She talked to you?" Liliha asked. She hadn't heard Kalani say a coherent sentence since Hana, Martha, and the minister had carried the woman from the *pali* to the hospital. Occasionally, Kalani managed a curse flung like acid.

"Yes, she talked."

"She knew what she was saying?"

Hana pondered for a moment, her gaze far away, her hands moving automatically as she swabbed the man's skin. "I think so. I don't believe she was delirious."

Liliha tried to imagine Kalani with flowing black hair, thick to her waist. Impossible. She shook herself, glanced back at Hana, whispered, "But she doesn't have any hair *now*."

"She hacked it off with a knife after she came to Molokai."

"Yes," Liliha answered slowly. "I'd heard that."

"She was in the very first group sent here. Did you know *that*?"

Shaking her head, Liliha gazed at Kalani again. It astonished her how Hana talked about Kalani so casually, like she was just another person, just another wretch sentenced to Kalaupapa.

"She wanted to make herself as ugly as she could—and as strong. So the men shipped here wouldn't . . ." Hana paused. "So they wouldn't take advantage of her. One man did, I guess, and she was determined no one else would ever do that to her again."

"But—?"

"The more she looked like a man, the safer she thought she was. The more she fought and made people fear her, the less *she* had to fear."

Liliha rubbed her forehead, trying to understand. "So—she was *afraid*?"

Hana smiled, her plump cheeks dimpling. "Of course she was. Just like everyone else who comes here."

"Not you, though."

Hana's smile broadened, lit her eyes. "Oh, yes, me, too. I'm afraid sometimes. Aren't you?"

"Yes."

"And didn't you used to be scared sometimes even when you were still at home?"

Liliha pressed her fingertips hard together, stared at the floor. She remembered her grandmother spewing curses at her, her uncle yelling that she was stupid and slow. She remembered her mother's sad eyes, how they flattened with defeat, how she urged Liliha into Grandmother's house—"Just for a little while, just a few more days"—and hunched silently into Uncle Malietoa's hut to mend his clothes and cook his meals.

"Either no place is safe," Hana said, standing, "or every place *is*."

Kalani turned onto her back, closed her eyes, lashes crusty and white. Her face was stiff and flat as the blunt end of an oar. Liliha shivered.

"Her eyes need bathing," Hana said, submerging the cloth in the water bucket Liliha had returned. Liliha now fetched her own water in a pail that the Captain left behind after he'd resigned as superintendent a month earlier. Manukekua had "loaned" it to her permanently.

Hana wrung out the rag and extended it toward Liliha.

Liliha's fingers brushed the cloth. It was cool. She drew her hand back.

Hana nodded. "That's all right," she said as she dabbed at Kalani's eyelashes. "She said she saved the hair after she cut it off. She hid it in her hut."

Liliha waited, but Hana didn't speak, only continued to swab Kalani's eyes, rinsed the cloth, and wiped the woman's face clean.

Even at a distance, Liliha could see the odd tilt of the walls and a ragged gash where part of the grass roof had collapsed. The man who'd helped guard the hut had kept it for himself after Kalani's accident. But he'd had only days to enjoy it before his lungs gave way to pneumonia. He'd crawled halfway to Kalawao, apparently looking for help, and had died alone, curled up on a barren stretch of ground. Other people had been to the hut already and they'd managed to just about destroy the place. On the hard earth worn bare in front of the door lay the remains of a red clay plate, the shards filmed with fine dust. Liliha picked up a fragment. The edge was sharp and smooth, like a tooth.

A noise inside the hut made Liliha grip the shard. She leaned toward the door, listened to a scuffing on the floor, and someone muttering.

Liliha took a deep breath and sliced into the hut with a single, long stride.

"Nothing." The word rasped in the gloom. "All this way. It took me all day to walk over here and it'll be dark by the time I walk all the way back. And for what?" Pauahi glanced at Liliha with sour eyes. "You might help me get outside, you know."

After a moment's hesitation, Liliha reached forward. Dropping the clay fragment, her fingers closed instead around a withered arm, an elbow sharp as an arrowhead. She could smell Pauahi's skin, a mixture of worn leather and salt.

Outside, Pauahi sank to the ground. She squinted up at Liliha and her eyes glinted greedily as ever.

"There's nothing left. Nothing worth a person's time anyway." Pauahi's lumpish foot stubbed at a fragment of the plate. "It's been picked at already. And people coming in there at night to sleep. Or whatever. It stinks of them."

"You walked here by yourself?" Liliha asked.

"Of course by myself. Do you see anybody else?"

Shaking her head, Liliha leaned inside the hut again.

"It's no good. I told you, there's nothing left. Not that you were the best helper I ever had, but even you were better than that miserable Opuhumanuu."

A moment's pause. *"Who?"* Liliha said.

"Opuhumanuu." Fingers dug petulantly at Liliha's leg. "She's worthless. Can barely carry *one* water bucket. Oh, she brought me a few of Kalani's things, but she let a whole pack of thieves come in here and take what they could carry off. I don't trust that one." Pauahi's eyes were slits, tinged yellow. "She said everything was gone, picked over, but how can anyone believe a word that miserable dwarf says? And to think, she wouldn't have a roof over her head or a bite to eat if it wasn't for *my* generosity. Not that she's grateful."

"Hmm," Liliha grunted, peering inside, searching, her eyes growing accustomed to the gloom.

Pauahi was relentless. "So I walked all the way here—hours, *hours,* and look at my feet, they're bleeding. And what do I find? Nothing."

Liliha started across the room. What was that on the other side, wedged against the wall?

"Now, look." Pauahi's whine followed her inside. "We might be able to work out a bargain. You weren't so bad at fishing. And I wouldn't swear to it, but I think you were honest with the rations. First thing, you can get me back to my house."

Liliha covered her ears, but Pauahi's voice was impossible to block out entirely. "You're strong yet. No reason you couldn't help me back. And my supply of water's getting low."

Liliha crouched. One hand touched dust and rotting ribbon.

"I won't give you another chance. Liliha!" She heard Pauahi spit into the dirt. "You're as ungrateful as that other one." A pause that Liliha barely noticed and then a voice thick with venom. "Just don't ever expect any more favors from *me*." Pauahi's blunt feet thudded against the ground, retreating.

Liliha moved to the doorway, raising her hand into the light.

Gray dust fuzzed the long switch of hair. A yellow ribbon lashed into a tight bow at one end was dull and soiled. The ragged ends of hair escaping above the bow showed that the hair had been chopped, brutally hacked. Closing her eyes, Liliha tried to see Kalani, sweating with fear, face not yet deformed, one hand holding her ponytail out from her scalp while the other hand sawed at it with a knife. Had she cried when she cut it? Or thought about how far she was from home, wondered how her life had taken such a strange turn? When had she started to enjoy the power of making other people afraid, of hurting them? Liliha thought about how she'd wanted to kill Kalani, the surge of satisfaction she'd felt when she fractured Kalani's ribs and knocked out her tooth. How easy would it be to make the same choices Kalani made, to become just like her?

Liliha drew her arm back, started to toss the hair back where she'd found it, but stopped in midthrow. Instead, she wound the hair into a coil and tucked it under the waist of her skirt. She would take it to Hana later, let Hana decide what to do with it.

When she went outside, she saw lepers creeping along the road. She broke into an awkward trot. Someone must have sighted a ship. Did Manukekua know? Even without Kalani around to steal rations, it was still crucial to get to the shipments early and to watch with a sharp eye. Kalaupapa suffered no shortage of bullies and thieves, but at least none of them bore a particular grudge against Liliha. She veered from the road. Manukekua was building a hut for himself inland, not too far from where Liliha lived, though he still stayed at the Captain's house each night to keep squatters from ruining it before the new superintendent arrived. The Captain had escaped on the last ship, mute and stiff-faced, never looking back at Kalaupapa or the *pali*, but staring straight out to sea. He'd taken with him the spoon with the handle carved like a ship.

Liliha hadn't gone far when she saw Manukekua loping toward her. When he spotted her, he grinned. A puckered scar angled from his hairline down to where his right eyebrow used to be.

"A ship's come!" Liliha shouted, one hand cupping her mouth.

He nodded, hurrying toward her. They fell into step along the road.

"We'll have to get rations for Hana, too," Liliha said.

"They don't like giving food to a *kōkua*. Especially since the person she came with is dead and she can go back home if she isn't sick."

"We'll get the rations," Liliha said quietly. She closed her eyes, breathed in deeply. She didn't like to think about Hana's leaving. The air felt fresh and clean, pouring into her lungs. She opened her eyes, glanced at Manukekua. A fresh sore, narrow and long and oddly rippled along one edge, shone near his jaw. Liliha thought of the fluted edge of a wet shell.

She drew closer to him. "I've been thinking," she said.

"About what?"

"That letter to my mother."

His expression held steady, waiting.

"I was thinking maybe I should send another one. Try to."

His smile disappeared. "Liliha—"

She held a hand toward him. "Not the same kind of letter. Different. Just to let her know that . . ." She looked down at her shoes stumping clumsily on the dirt. "That I'm all right. This time, it might actually get to her."

"Hana would carry it for you," Manukekua said. "If she decides to leave."

"Yes."

"She still didn't say for sure?"

"No. It's hard for her, going to the hospital and trying to help people and then not having enough bandages or medicine or food. But she says they need a nurse more here than Honolulu ever could. So maybe she'll stay."

They walked quietly, Liliha's shoes scuffing the dirt, until Manukekua squeezed her arm. "Come on," he said. "Race you."

She pushed his hand away and broke into an uneven gallop. They hurtled past the other people limping toward Kalaupapa landing. Liliha's hair flew behind her. Her numb feet and the shoes slowed her, but how good it felt to *run*. Not to worry about being careful, not to worry about falling down or making her feet worse.

Manukekua reached the edge of the ocean just seconds before Liliha. He kicked his feet in the water.

"I wish I could do that," Liliha said, jerking her chin at his feet. "Walk on shells and rocks." She grimaced. *"Shoes."* She spoke the word like a dark curse.

They watched as rowboats sprouted from the ship and surged toward shore.

"Here." Manukekua spread his arms out.

Liliha looked at him, puzzled.

"You can take your shoes off."

She bent down and slowly unfastened one shoe at the ankle. Manukekua helped her until both shoes were loose and she could pull them off. He wrapped his arms around her and lifted her above the ground. Although his arms were thin, they were strong. He carried her out to where a boulder sat, black and squat as one of those trolls in the stories the Scottish doctor had told Liliha. The boulder was smooth. Manukekua settled her on it, then sat beside her. Liliha's feet dangled in the water.

"Can you feel it?" Manukekua asked.

She swished her legs back and forth. The water was warm against her calves; it splashed at her knees. Then, just for an instant, it was as if the sole of her right foot touched a swathe of cool silk. Liliha gasped and leaned forward. The water was murky, grains of sand and bits of shell churning up from the bottom. And something else.

A dark shape, black at first, then gray, rose toward her. Near the surface, it glittered, its scales a thousand silver sparks. An *aholeahole*. A bright, beautiful fish. She hadn't seen one since she left home. Liliha watched in amazement and pushed her hands into the water.

The fish streamed past her fingers. Liliha didn't try to catch it, somehow didn't *want* to catch it. Even after it sank back into the dark water and vanished, Liliha could still feel the cool, slippery scales on her fingers.

She splashed her hands and legs through the water and laughed. Oh, even if it was all her imagination, she didn't care. It was too wonderful, feeling something cool and smooth with the sole of her foot, with her fingers, with skin that had been as good as dead.

"They're coming," Manukekua said. The boats bucked past, nearly ashore. They were crowded, not only with the usual sailors and crates, but also with a dozen or more lepers and, at the prow of the first boat, a short man with a sharp, worried face, shiny brown skin, and a plain dark jacket and trousers.

"That must be him," Manukekua said. "The new superintendent." He swung off the boulder and carried her, staggering just a little, onto the beach.

"He's Hawaiian?" Liliha said, shoving her wet feet into her boots and fastening the buttons as best she could, muttering impatiently at the blunt clumsiness of her fingers.

"He looks it," Manukekua said, bending over to finish fastening her shoes. No sooner had the new superintendent stepped from the boat than a crowd of twisted faces and deformed bodies massed around him. Everyone seemed to be speaking at once, including the superintendent.

Manukekua headed for the crates, where another mob scuffled under a sailor's bored gaze. Liliha started after him, then stopped.

The new arrivals had stumbled from the boats into ankle-deep water, and now Liliha watched them stagger ashore. Their backs slumped and their arms dangled with exhaustion. Some of them gaped at the mob of lepers swarming over the supply crates; others, heads slung back, stared at the forbidding height of the *pali*. A few turned their heads from side to side, as if trying to understand this strange, new place, but they might as well have been blind. Their eyes were blank, uncomprehending, alone.

Manukekua stopped, reaching one hand back toward Liliha.

"Go ahead," she said, and waved in the direction of the crates. "I'll catch up."

He hesitated, then nodded. "I'll find enough for both of us. And Hana." When he neared the crates, he slipped into the crowd.

A boy, about ten years old, with a short, chunky body and stout legs, rubbed his eyes and gawked at Liliha. She bent forward, just enough so that her eyes were level with his. She didn't try to take his hand or touch his shoulder. She didn't smile either, for that would have seemed like a lie.

He swiped at his eyes again, a quick, angry motion. "They didn't tell us anything," he said. Tears glittered on the back of his hand.

"What's your name?" Liliha asked.

"Keoua." His voice tightened with fear. "Why won't they tell us anything?" Anger made his shoulders tremble. "Nobody asked me if I *wanted* to come here."

"No," Liliha said. "Nobody asks that. But I'll tell you about this place." He looked at her with sudden astonishment, and she didn't know why until she realized, with equal amazement, that she *was* smiling at him.

"My name is Liliha. And this . . ." She turned inland, swept one hand across the peninsula. The boy's eyes darted from the crooked thumb on her right hand to the *pali*, which glowed a fierce green in the afternoon sun. Fear caught his eyes and pulled at his mouth, easing only when he turned back to Liliha's face and her smile.

"And this," she said again, "is Kalaupapa."

Hawaiian Words

Ahi (ah'-hee)—most commonly refers to the yellowfin tuna, which has a delicate white meat when cooked. When Hawaiians pulled ahi onto their canoes, the fish would sometimes make such desperate attempts to get away that the fishing line would rub against the wooden canoe and smoke.

Ahia (ah-hee'-ah)

Aholeahole (ah-ho'-leh-ah-ho'-leh)—a fish, easily growing a foot long or more, used as food. The name means "sparkly." Another common name for this fish is the flagtail.

'Awa (ah'-wah or ah'-vah)—black-colored plant used for ceremonial and medicinal purposes. Generally, the root would be chewed to form several small balls, which would then be mixed with water and other ingredients. The solid particles were ultimately removed from the mixture and the remaining liquid consumed. 'Awa was used for toothaches, insomnia, headaches, and other illnesses.

Hana (hah'-nah)

Haole (how'-leh)—a Caucasian, usually an American or English person. Formerly used to refer to any foreigner.

Heiau (hay'-ow)—a site for worship in the native, pre-Christian religion. Remains show that a heiau could be a building or altar, a stone platform, or a terrace made of earth.

I'iwi (ee'-ee'-vee)—a bird, also called a honeycreeper, found on all the main islands. It has bright red feathers, a pink, curved bill, black wings, and a black tail. Its call has been described as sounding like the squeak of two balloons being rubbed together.

Imu (ee'-moo)—an underground oven.

'Iwa (ee'-vah)—the great frigate bird, a large, wide-winged flyer of the tropical seas known for snatching food from other birds in midair. The 'iwa built nests in bushes or other vegetation and, when flying, could soar for hours on updrafts.

Kalani (kah'-lah'-nee)

Kama'āina (kahm'-uh-ī'-nuh)—native-born. The original residents of a place.

Kapa (kah'-pah)—cloth made from the bark of various plants.

Kī (kee)—a woody plant of the lily family. Kī plants have slender stems and clusters of narrow leaves as long as one or two feet and produce small, light flowers. Kī leaves were used for thatching, food wrappers, hula skirts, sandals, and other items.

Kiawe (kee-yah'-veh)—the algaroba tree. This legume from tropical America was first planted in Hawaii in 1828, but soon became very common. It grows well in dry areas and is an important shade tree.

Koa (koh'-wah)—a large native forest tree with crescent-shaped leaves and white flowers that appear in small, round heads. It produces a fine red wood used to make canoes, surfboards, calabashes, ukeleles, and other items.

Kōkua (koh-koo'-uh)—a helper who accompanied a leper into exile.

Kukui (koo'-kwee)—this large tree is also called the candlenut because its nuts contain white, oily kernels that were used as sources of light. Different parts of the kukui also provided medicine, dye, fuel, and food.

Lei (lay)—a string of flowers placed around the neck and used for greetings or to honor a person's status.

Liliha (lee-lee'-hah)

Mahimahi (mah'-hee-mah'-hee)—also known as the dolphin fish. A mahimahi is *not* a dolphin. Mahimahi, found throughout tropical waters, are surface feeders that sometimes gather around buoys, logs, or other floating objects to eat the smaller fish they find there. When caught, mahimahi usually weigh about eight to twenty-five pounds and are still considered a delicious variety of fish to eat.

Ma'i pākē (mah'-ee pah'-kay)—Chinese disease. A term used for leprosy since some believed that the Chinese brought the disease to the islands.

Makai (muh-kī')—toward the sea.

Malietoa (mahl'-yeh-toh'-wah)

Malo (mah'-loh)—a loincloth.

Manini (mah-nee'-nee)—a fish that lives primarily in coral reefs, tide-pools, and shallow water. It is also called the convict tang because it has six vertical black stripes that look like old-fashioned prison clothes. Growing to a length of seven or eight inches, these fish could be caught in throw nets and were eaten either raw or dried.

Manukekua (mah'-nooh-keh-koo'-ah)

Mauka (mao'-kuh)—inland.

Naio (ni'-oh)—a native plant that varies from a shrub at low elevations to a tall tree at higher elevations. It has dark green, narrow leaves that are pointed at the ends. The bark is very dark, and the wood is hard enough that it could be used to build frames for traditional huts. The wood's oil smells much like sandalwood.

'O'ili (oh-ee'-lee)—the fantail file fish, endemic to Hawaii. The full Hawaiian name is *'o'ili-'uwi'uwi*. This fish is yellow with black spots and has a growth on the top of its head that looks like a horn. It is commonly found in shallow waters.

Olona (oh-loh'-nah)—a native shrub with large, fine-toothed leaves. The bark was used to make a strong fiber for fishing nets and as a base for kī-leaf raincoats and feather capes.

O'o (oh'-oh')—also known as the honeyeater, this bird is black with yellow feathers tufted under each wing. Its feathers were used extensively as decoration.

Opuhumanuu (oh'-poo-hoo'-mah-noo'-oo)

Pa'i 'ai (pah'-ee eye')—hard, pounded taro that has not been diluted with water. Stored in hard blocks, pa'i 'ai could be transported easily and later cooked with water to make poi.

Painiu (pi'-new)—a native Hawaiian lily with long, narrow, silvery leaves and fleshy, orange fruits. It is most often found in moist, forested areas.

Pali (pah'-lee)—cliff; precipice.

Pauahi (pow-ah'-hee)

Pawale (pah-wah'-leh or pah-vah'-leh)—a shrubby plant growing as high as four feet tall. It produces fruits and clusters of small red flowers. This plant grows in wet forests on Molokai, Maui, and Hawaii.

Pili (pee'-lee)—a type of grass found in many warm regions. Used as thatch.

Poi (poy)—a staple of the Hawaiian diet. It is a paste made from taro root by cooking and pounding the root and mixing it with water. Poi can be eaten fresh or fermented for a more sour taste. Traditionally, it would be eaten by an entire family, using their fingers, from a single large bowl.

Pueo (poo-ay'-oh)—the Hawaiian short-eared owl, present on all the Hawaiian islands. The pueo grows to be thirteen to seventeen inches long, has brown and white feathers, and is often active during the day. These owls were traditionally held in high regard as guardians and signs of good fortune.

Pū hala (poo' hah'-lah)—a tree also known as the hala, pandanus, or screwpine. It grows both wild and under cultivation. Slanting aerial roots grow around the base of the trunk. The branches are tipped with narrow, spine-edged leaves. Different parts of the tree were used to make mats, baskets, hats, leis, and medicine.

Taro (tar'-oh)—traditional vegetable eaten by Hawaiians and a staple of their diet. Taro, also called kalo, has long leaves shaped like arrowheads and stems that can rise a foot or more in height. Different varieties grow best either in uplands or in wet, marshy areas. All parts of the plant can be eaten, but the most important part is the root, which is used to make poi.

'Ulili (ooh-lee'-lee)—also called the wandering tatler. These migrant birds prefer to be around water, including inland streams. They are gray with darker bars and streaks ornamenting the feathers, dull yellow legs, and white rings around their eyes. Their call sounds like their Hawaiian name.

Ulua (oo'-loo-wah)—the jack or jackfish. These fish were important sources of food to Hawaiians. They are deepwater bottom fish, usually about ten to forty pounds when caught, but with the potential to grow to be one hundred pounds.

HISTORICAL NOTE

No one knows for certain when the dreaded scourge of leprosy first appeared in the Hawaiian Islands, although there is speculation that the disease arrived by 1830. The native Hawaiians sometimes called the ailment *ma'i pākē,* the Chinese Disease, in the belief that Chinese laborers brought leprosy with them. The disease was also known as *ma'i ali'i,* the Royal Sickness, referring to a Hawaiian chief who allegedly contracted the disease while traveling abroad and then returned home to spread the contagion.

As the disease intensified among the population, an alarmed government took action. In 1865 the Legislative Assembly passed "An Act to Prevent the Spread of Leprosy." The government procured Makanalua peninsula, commonly known as Kalaupapa, on the northern tip of Molokai and established a leper colony there in 1866. Why Kalaupapa? The 2,000-foot *pali* and rough shores isolated the peninsula and made contact with the outside world difficult. *Taro,* sweet potatoes, and other foods could be cultivated on the flat terrain and fresh water was available, if hard to obtain. Laws required that all lepers be exiled to Kalaupapa in order to keep the rest of the population safe. Kalihi Hospital and Detention Station was constructed approximately two miles from Honolulu; there, doctors examined suspected lepers and determined their fates.

The government initially planned that the lepers would support themselves, not realizing that the sick were too demoralized, disabled, and weak to farm, fish, tend livestock, or build houses. "As more people arrived, housing, food, and water procurement problems multiplied. Quarrels arose easily and due to the lack of sufficient supervision, were settled among the people themselves, sometimes violently" (*Exile in Paradise,* p. 54). Even the climate proved difficult. The peninsula's northern location and high cliffs brought cool temperatures. Frequent rainstorms and high winds made the sick all the more wretched.

Kalaupapa quickly became so notorious that some leprosy victims tried to hide in the forests and mountainous countryside of their home islands to avoid detection. Relatives often sheltered the sick and attempted to protect them from the authorities. A few lepers went so far as to kill police officers rather than face exile. Lepers living on Kalaupapa in the settlement's early years confronted enormous difficulties. Food rations were often insufficient and the walk required to obtain those rations must have been daunting to anyone suffering from such a debilitating disease. Fetching water also demanded an arduous trek. Housing was insufficient and medical care practically nonexistent. Too often despair and lawlessness reigned. "In this place there is no law" was reported to be the greeting given to newcomers during those terrible years. An 1868 report by the Board of Health to the Legislative Assembly describes the situation:

> [T]he terrible disease which afflicts the Lepers seems to cause among them as great a change in their moral and mental organization as in their physical constitution; so far from aiding their weaker brethren, the strong took possession of everything, devoured and destroyed the large quantity of food on the lands, and altogether refused to replant anything; indeed, they had no compunction in taking from those who were disabled and dying, the material supplies of clothes and food which were dispensed by the Superintendent for the use of the latter; they exhibited the most thorough indifference to the sufferings, and the utter absence of consideration for the wants, to which many of them were destined to be themselves exposed in perhaps a few weeks; in fact, the most of those in whom the disease had progressed considerably,

showed the greatest thoughtlessness and heartlessness. [*Exile in Paradise,* pp. 54–55]

In the period from 1866 to 1873, approximately forty percent of the lepers at Kalaupapa died.

Descriptions of individuals written by doctors of the time provide striking images of the physical debilitation of the victims:

> Rebecca—Female . . . Admitted March 9, 1883; aged 12, sick 6 years . . . Apparently healthy until 6 years old. Had sores on the private parts, and nose supperated. Bubos came and went. Had small-pox which caused loss of joint of fingers and pieces of bones in others, leaving the distorted, enlarged white-pink scars. At the present time there is a total loss of eyebrows, loss of soft palate; cannot speak loud; tubercles on lobes of ears and cheeks; end of nose sore; numerous scars on legs and knees; the skin of the leg is dark, dry, shining, and cracked; tongue cracked . . . Died 1886. [*Path of the Destroyer,* p. 166]

> Stephen Kiwaa—Male; admitted March 10, 1883; aged 23 . . . Loss of bones from toes of left foot; plantar ulcers right and left. Anaesthesia of both forearms up to the elbows. Eyes watery and lower lids drawn down. Atrophy. Paralysis of left face well marked . . . Had many bad sores on entire body when 6 years old with scabby eruptions when very small. Hopeless. Molokai. [*Path of the Destroyer,* p. 164]

Perhaps just as terrible as the physical corruption caused by the disease was the exile imposed on its victims. A man, looking back from the vantage point of the late 1970s, remembered it this way:

> One of the worst things about this illness is what was done to me as a young boy. First, I was sent away from my family. That was hard. I was so sad to go to Kalaupapa. They told me

right out that I would die here; that I would never see my family again. I heard them say this phrase, something I will never forget. They said, "This is your last place. This is where you are going to stay, and die." That's what they told me. I was a thirteen-year-old kid. [Kalaupapa National Historical Park]

Liliha's religious confusion reflects her rapidly changing culture. American Protestant missionaries arrived in Hawaii in 1820, followed seven years later by the first Catholics. At the order of King Liholiho, images of the traditional gods were burned and *heiaus* (traditional temples) destroyed. Changes were not limited to the realm of religion. Nineteenth-century photographs amply demonstrate a society in transition. Some men wear the traditional *malo* (loincloth) while others don trousers and jackets or elaborate military-style uniforms. Pictures show women dressed in Hawaiian capes or simple, loose dresses, puffed blouses tucked into full skirts or, in the case of royalty, elaborate evening gowns. Even in the late 1800s there were still fishermen heading out to sea in outrigger canoes, traditional foods cooked in earth ovens, and occasional grass houses featuring decidedly *un*-traditional windows and tall doorways. The Hawaiian Islands became a convenient port for ships crossing the Pacific; the contact with outsiders meant new tools, manufactured goods, weapons, industries, foods, plants, animals, and—unfortunately—new diseases.

The characters in this novel are fictitious. An old sea captain *did* serve as assistant to a superintendent named Mrs. Walsh in the late 1860s, but his depiction in this story (and his promotion to superintendent) is primarily my own invention. The sea captain could not speak the language of the native people. Eventually, after a brief rebellion on the part of the sick, a native Hawaiian was given the position of superintendent. However, it was not until the arrival of a Catholic priest named Father Damien in 1873 that conditions significantly improved. Damien's writings provide details about Kalaupapa that bring the place powerfully to life. For example, he notes that the smell of the diseased was so terrible that he would smoke a pipe when he went into the houses in an effort to keep the stench out of his nostrils.

At its peak in 1890, more than 1,000 people lived at Kalaupapa. Sulfone drugs introduced in 1946 alleviated leprosy symptoms. At last, those who contracted the disease could hope for a more normal life. In 1980, Kalaupapa became a National Historic Park. Approximately forty-five people who have leprosy, now called Hansen's Disease, continue to live there, although no laws require them to stay.

As of 1997, the World Health Organization reported the number of identified leprosy cases worldwide as 890,000, with seventy percent of the patients found in India, Indonesia, and Myanamar (Burma). Drugs are now available that, administered over a period ranging from six months to more than two years, halt the disease. However, any deformities or nerve damage already suffered by the patient are not curable. Physicians may recommend reconstructive surgery, if available, to try to correct deformities. Patients must learn to take care of numb arms and legs and have to check themselves frequently for cuts, which could become infected. Special exercises help them to maintain good movement of their joints. Some patients must wear special footwear to prevent or alleviate foot ulcers.

I consulted a number of books in researching this novel. The two most useful and fascinating were *Exile in Paradise: The Isolation of Hawaii's Leprosy Victims and Development of Kalaupapa Settlement, 1865 to the Present* and *Path of the Destroyer*. Both quote extensively from documents of the period. To read them is to immerse oneself in the full confusion and terror of Kalaupapa's beginnings.